"Was It Real, What We Felt Then?"

A long sigh shuddered through him before he spoke. "Real enough that we went through a lot of pain for each other. Real enough that sitting here together isn't some easygoing reunion."

Hearing that heavy sigh of his, she realized he'd suffered, too, more than she'd ever known. Somehow, that made her feel less alone. Yes, they'd hurt each other, but maybe they could help each other, too. Maybe the time had come for a coda of sorts, to bring their song to an end.

"Malcolm, what's Europe going to be like if just sitting here together is this difficult?"

"So you've decided to come with me? No more maybes."

She shoved to her feet and walked to him at the piano. "I think I have to."

"Because of the stalker?"

She cupped his handsome, beard-stubbled face in her hands. "Because it's time we put this to rest."

Before she could talk herself out of something she wanted—needed—more than air, Celia pressed her lips to his.

Dear Reader,

My family is full of couples who married their high school sweetheart. There's undoubtedly something special about that first love, as the hero and heroine in *Playing for Keeps* know all too well. Although, Malcolm and Celia had to wait through many years and heartaches to find the happily-ever-after they were destined to enjoy. I had a blast penning their journey!

For those of you who enjoy connected stories, *Playing for Keeps* is book three in my Alpha Brotherhood series (although it can be read as a stand-alone). If you would like to read the earlier books—*An Inconvenient Affair* and *All or Nothing*—both are still available online. Also, Alpha Brotherhood book four will feature Dr. Rowan Boothe and be part of Harlequin Desire's Billionaires and Babies program in October 2013.

I've been thrilled with the reader response to my Alpha Brotherhood series. Your emails and posts online make for such an awesome treat when I take a break from writing to play on the internet. Thank you from the bottom of my heart!

Happy reading!

Cheers,

Cathy

Catherine Mann
Website: CatherineMann.com
Facebook: www.facebook.com/CatherineMannAuthor
Twitter: twitter.com/CatherineMann1

CATHERINE MANN

PLAYING FOR KEEPS

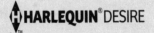

Recycling programs
for this product may
not exist in your area.

ISBN-13: 978-0-373-73234-0

PLAYING FOR KEEPS

Printed in U.S.A.

HARLEQUIN®
www.Harlequin.com

Books by Catherine Mann

Harlequin Desire

Acquired: The CEO's Small-Town Bride #2090
Billionaire's Jet Set Babies #2115
Honorable Intentions #2151
***An Inconvenient Affair* #2173
**All or Nothing #2203

Silhouette Desire

Baby, I'm Yours #1721
Under the Millionaire's Influence #1787
The Executive's Surprise Baby #1837
**Rich Man's Fake Fiancée* #1878
*His Expectant Ex #1895
Propositioned Into a Foreign Affair #1941
**Millionaire in Command* #1969
Bossman's Baby Scandal #1988
**The Tycoon Takes a Wife* #2013
Winning It All #2031
  "Pregnant with the Playboy's Baby"
†*The Maverick Prince* #2047
†*His Thirty-Day Fiancée* #2061
†*His Heir, Her Honor* #2071

*The Landis Brothers
†Rich, Rugged & Royal
**The Alpha Brotherhood

Other titles by this author available in ebook format.

CATHERINE MANN

USA TODAY bestselling author Catherine Mann lives on a sunny Florida beach with her flyboy husband and their four children. With more than forty books in print in over twenty countries, she has also celebrated wins for both a RITA® Award and a Booksellers' Best Award. Catherine enjoys chatting with readers online—thanks to the wonders of the internet, which allows her to network with her laptop by the water! Contact Catherine through her website, www.catherinemann.com, find her on Facebook and Twitter (@CatherineMann1) or reach her by snail mail at P.O. Box 6065, Navarre, FL 32566.

To the charter members of "The Tree House Club," karaoke singers extraordinaire:
Johnny, Tom, Elena, Lori, Mike, Vicky, George, Jerry, Linda, Shawn, Chris, and Daphne.

One

Midway through the junior-high choir's rehearsal of "It's a Small World," Celia Patel found out just how small the world could shrink.

She dodged left and right as half the singers—the female half—sprinted down the stands, squealing in fangirl glee. Their footsteps rattled metal risers and squeaked on the gymnasium floor, the stampeding herd moving as one. All their energy focused on racing to the back of the gymnasium where *he* stood.

Malcolm Douglas.

Seven-time Grammy award winner.

Platinum-selling soft-rock star.

And the man who'd broken Celia's heart when they were both sixteen years old.

Celia hefted aside her music stand before the last of the middle-school girls rushed by, oblivious to her attempts to stop them. Identical twins Valentina and Valeria nearly plowed her down in their dash to the back. Already, a couple dozen students circled him. Two body-guards shuffled their feet uncertainly while more squeals and giggles ricocheted into the rafters.

Malcolm raised a stalling hand to the ominous body-guards while keeping his eyes locked on Celia, smiling that million-watt grin that had graced CD covers and promo shots. Tall and honed, he still had a hometown-boy-handsome appeal that hadn't dimmed. He'd merely matured—now polished with confidence and about twenty more pounds of whipcord muscle.

Success and chart-topping wealth probably didn't hurt.

She wanted him gone. For her sanity's sake, she *needed* him gone. But now that he was here, she couldn't look away.

He wore his khakis and designer loafers—sockless—with the easy confidence of a man comfortable in his skin. Sleeves rolled up on his chambray shirt exposed strong, tanned forearms and musician's hands.

Best not to think about his talented, nimble hands.

His sandy-brown hair was as thick as she remembered. It was still a little long, skimming over his forehead in a way that once called to her fingers to stroke it back. And those blue eyes—heaven help her—she recalled well how indigo-dark they went just before he kissed her with the enthusiasm and ardor of a hormone-pumped teenager.

There was no denying he was all man now.

What in the hell was he doing here? Malcolm hadn't set foot in Azalea, Mississippi, since a judge crony of her father's had offered Malcolm the choice of juvie or military reform school nearly eighteen years ago. Since he'd left her behind—scared, *pregnant* and determined to salvage her life.

Even though he showed up regularly in the tabloids,

seeing him in person after all these years was different. Not that she'd gone searching for photos of him. But given his popularity, she couldn't help but be periodically blindsided by glimpses of him. Worst of all, though, was hearing the sound of his voice crooning over the radio as she changed the station.

Now, across the room, he pressed a paper against his knee to sign an autograph for Valentina—or Valeria. No one could tell them apart, not even their mother sometimes. Totally beside the point, because watching Malcolm with the young girl twisted Celia's heart with what could have been if somehow, against the odds and all better judgment, they'd been able to keep and raise their baby.

But they weren't sixteen anymore, and she'd put aside reckless dreams the day she'd handed her newborn daughter over to a couple who could give the precious child everything Celia and Malcolm couldn't.

She threw back her shoulders and started toward the cluster across the gym, determined to get through this surprise visit with her pride in place. At least the nine boys in the choir were sitting on the risers, making the most of the chance to play with video games banned during class. She let that slide for now and zeroed in on the mini-mob collected by a rolling cart full of basketballs just under a red exit sign.

"Class, we need to give Mr. Douglas some breathing room." She closed in on the circle of girls, resisting the urge to smooth her hands down her sunshine-yellow sundress. She gently tapped Sarah Lynn Thompson's wrist. "And no pulling hair to sell online, girls."

Sarah Lynn dropped her hand to her side, a guilty flush spreading up her face.

Malcolm passed back the last of the autographs and

tucked the pen in his shirt pocket. "I'm fine, Celia, but thanks for making sure I don't go prematurely bald."

"Celia? *Celia?*" asked Valeria. Or was it Valentina? "Miss Patel, you know him? Oh, my God! How? Why didn't you tell us?"

She didn't intend to delve too deeply into those murky waters. "We went to high school together." His name was etched on the sign that proclaimed "Welcome to Azalea, Home of Malcolm Douglas" as if the town hadn't once tried to send him to jail because of her. "Now, let's get back to the risers, and I'm sure Mr. Douglas will answer your questions in an orderly fashion since he disrupted our rehearsal."

She shot him a censorious look that merely prompted an unrepentant grin in return.

Sarah Lynn stayed glued to Celia's side. "Did you two date?"

The bell rang—thank God—signaling the end of class and no time for questions after all. "Students, line up for your last class."

And wouldn't you know, both the principal and the secretary stood in the doorway as starstruck as their students in spite of the fact that both ladies were happily married and grandmothers. How had he gotten into the gym/auditorium without causing a riot?

Celia led the students to the double door, her sandals slapping the wood floor. Step by step, she realized the pair of guards inside were only a part of Malcolm's security detail. Four more muscle-bound men stood outside in the hallway while a large limo lurked beyond the glassed front entrance. Additional cars with majorly tinted windows were parked in front of and behind the stretch limo.

Malcolm shook hands with the principal and secretary, making small talk as he introduced himself, ironic as all get-out since at least half of the free world knew his face. "I'll leave autographed photos for your students."

Sarah Lynn called over her shoulder, dragging her feet on the way down the hall, "For all of us?"

"Miss Patel will let me know how many."

The last of the students stepped into the corridor, the door swooshing closed after the administrators left. How had their departure managed to suck all the air out of the massive gym along with them? She stood an arm's reach away from Malcolm, his two bodyguards looming just behind him.

So much for privacy.

"I assume you're here to see me?" Although she couldn't for the life of her fathom why.

"Yes, I am, darlin'," he drawled, his smooth baritone voice stroking over her senses like fine wine. "Is there somewhere we can talk without being interrupted?"

"Your security detail makes that rather moot, don't you think?" She smiled at the bulky duo, who stared back at her with such expressionless faces they could have been auditioning for positions as guards at Buckingham Palace.

Malcolm nodded to the stony-faced pair and without a word they both silently stepped out into the hall. "They'll stay outside the door, but they're here for your protection as much as mine."

"*My* protection?" She inched a step away to put a little distance between herself and the tempting scent of his aftershave. "I seriously doubt your fans will start worshipping me just because I knew you aeons ago."

"That's not what I meant." He scratched the back of his neck as if choosing his words carefully. "I hear via the grapevine there have been some threats made against you. A little extra security's a good thing, right?"

Perhaps some security from the temptation of having him around disrupting her well-ordered life, not to mention her hormones. "Thanks, but I'm good. It's just some crank calls and some strange notes. That kind of thing happens all too often when my dad has a high-profile case."

Although how in the world had Malcolm heard about it? Something uneasy shifted inside her, a stirring of panic she quickly squashed down. She refused to let Malcolm's appearance here yank the rug out from under her blessedly routine existence. She refused to give him the power to send her pulse racing.

Damn it all, she was a confident adult and this was her turf. Still, her nerves were as tight as piano strings. Fighting back the urge to snap at him for turning her world upside down, she folded her arms and waited. She wasn't an indulged, impulsive only child any longer. She wasn't a terrified, pregnant teen.

She wasn't a catatonic, broken young woman caught in the grips of a postpartum depression so deep her life had been at risk.

Her road back to peace had been hard-won with the help of the best shrinks money could buy. She refused to let anything or anyone—especially not Malcolm Douglas—threaten the future she'd built for herself.

Loving Celia Patel had changed his life forever. The jury was still out as to whether that had been a good or bad thing.

Regardless, their lives were linked. For nearly eighteen years, Malcolm had been able to keep his distance from her. But he'd never mastered the art of looking away, even when they were a couple of continents apart. Which was what had brought him here now, knowing too much about her life, too much about a threat to her safety that sent old protective urges into high gear. He just had to figure out how to persuade her to let him back into her life so he could help her. And by helping her, he could atone for how he'd wrecked their lives. Maybe then he could finally let go of a glorified puppy love that after so many years he doubted was real.

Although given his physical reaction to her at the moment, the memories of their attraction were 100 percent real. Once again, desire for Celia Patel threatened to knock him flat on his ass.

Hell, no, he hadn't been able to forget her even while across the world singing to sold-out stadiums. He certainly couldn't tear his eyes off her now when she walked only a step ahead. Her wavy dark hair hung loose halfway down her back, swaying with each step. The bright yellow sundress hugged her curves the way his hands once had.

He followed her across the gymnasium floor, the same building where they'd gone to school together. He'd performed on that stage in the junior-high choir to be with her. Taunts hadn't bothered him—until one stupid little idiot had said something off-color about Celia. Malcolm had decked him and gotten suspended for three days. Small price to pay. There was nothing he wouldn't do then for Celia.

Apparently that hadn't changed. One of his contacts had gotten wind of a case on her judge father's docket, a high-profile drug case with a kingpin who'd drawn a target on Celia's back. Malcolm had notified local authorities, but they hadn't bothered looking into the evidence he'd gifted them with. Evidence that detailed a money trail connecting a hit man to the suspected drug dealer.

Local authorities didn't like outsiders and were stubborn about their ability to handle matters on their own. Someone had to do something, and apparently that someone was Malcolm. Nothing, absolutely nothing, could derail him from his plan to protect Celia. He had to do this in order to make up for all the ways he'd let her down eighteen years ago.

She opened the door by the stage steps, her spine stiff and straight as she entered her small office lined with shelves surrounding a tiny desk. Musical scores and boxes of instruments packed the room—everything from triangles to xylophones to bongo drums. The smell of paper, ink and leather mixed with the familiar praline scent of Celia.

She spun to face him, her hair fanning gently, a strand caressing over his wrist. "It's more of a closet really, where I store my cart, instruments and paperwork. I travel from classroom to classroom, or we meet in the gym."

He adjusted the fit of his watch to cover rubbing away the sensation of her hair skimming his skin. "Just like the old days. Not much has changed here."

The police department was every bit as slack as before, swayed by the person with the most influence.

"Some things are different, Malcolm. *I* am different," she said in a cool tone he didn't recognize at all.

And he was a man who specialized in the timbre of the voice.

"Aren't you going to chew me out for disrupting your class?"

"That would be rude of me." Her fingers toyed restlessly with the ukulele on her desk, notes lightly filling the air. "Meeting you was obviously the highlight of their young lives."

"But obviously not the highlight of yours." Leaning back, he tucked his hands in his pockets to keep from stroking the strings along with her. Memories taunted him of how they'd played the guitar and piano together, their shared love of music leading to a shared love of each other's bodies. Had his mind exaggerated those memories into something more than they really were? So much time had passed since he'd seen her that he couldn't be sure.

"Why are you here?" The sight of her slim fingers moving along the strings damn near mesmerized him. "You don't have a performance scheduled in the area."

"You follow my tour schedule?" His eyes snapped up to her face.

She snorted on a laugh. "The whole freakin' town follows your every breath. What you eat for breakfast. Who you dated. I would have to be blind and deaf not to hear what the town has to say about their wonder boy. But personally? I'm no longer a charter member of the Malcolm Douglas fan club."

"Now, there's the Celia I remember." He grinned.

She didn't. "You still haven't answered my question. Why are you here?"

"I'm here for you." His libido shouted a resounding echo. Damn it all, why did she have to be even more lushly sensual now than she had been before?

"For me? I think not," she said coolly, her fingers still lightly stroking the ukulele with instinctive sensuality, as if she savored the feel of every note as much as the sound. "I have plans for tonight. You should have called ahead."

"You're much more level now than you were before."

Her expression flickered with something he couldn't quite grasp before she continued, "I was a teenager then. I'm an adult now, with adult responsibilities. So if we could speed this up, please?"

"You may not have kept track of my schedule, but I kept up with yours." He knew every detail of the threatening phone calls, the flat tire and the other threats increasing in frequency by the day. He also knew she'd only told her father half of what happened. The thought of each threat chilled Malcolm's ardor and ramped up his protectiveness. "I know you finished your music degree with honors from the University of Southern Mississippi. You've been teaching here since graduation."

"I'm proud of my life, thank you very much, far more than can be summed up in a couple of sentences. Did you come to give me a belated graduation gift? Because if not, you can go finish signing autographs."

"Let's cut to the chase, then." He shoved away from the door and stood toe-to-toe with her, just to prove to himself he could be near her and not haul her against him. "I came here to protect you."

Her fingers popped a string on the ukulele, and even though she didn't back away, her gaze skittered to the side. "Um, would you care to clarify?"

"You know full well what I'm talking about. Those crank calls you mentioned earlier." Why was she hiding the incidents from her old man? Anger nipped at his gut—at her for being reckless and at himself for having taken that tempting step closer. As if the room wasn't small enough already. "Your father's current case. Drug lord, kingpin. Ring a bell?"

"My father's a judge. He prosecutes bad guys and often they get angry, make empty threats." Her eyes met his again, any signs of unease gone, replaced with a poised distance so alien to the wild child she'd once been. "I'm not sure why this is your concern."

And there she'd hit on the truth. She wasn't his to watch over, but that didn't stop the urge to protect her any more than her dress could stop him from remembering what she looked like with only her long hair draped over her bare shoulders. His frustration snapped as surely as that nylon string. "Damn it, Celia, you're smarter than this."

Her plump lips pressed into a tight line. "Time for you to leave."

He gritted back his temper, recognizing it for what it was—frustrated desire. His attraction to her was even more powerful than he'd expected. "I apologize for being less than diplomatic. I heard about the threats on your life, and call me a nostalgic idiot, but I'm worried about you."

"How did you get the details?" Her face creased with confusion—and suspicion. "My father and I have made sure to keep everything out of the press."

"Dear old Dad may be a powerful judge, but his power doesn't reach everywhere."

"That doesn't explain how you found out."

He couldn't explain the "how" of that. There were things about him she didn't know. He kept much better secrets than her father. "But I'm right."

"One of the cases my father's prosecuting has gotten… messy. The police are investigating."

"You're really going to put your faith in the three-man shop they call a police department?" He couldn't keep the cynicism from his voice. "Security around you is awe-inspiring. I should get my men to make notes."

"No need to be sarcastic. I'm taking precautions. This isn't the first time someone has threatened our family because of my father's job."

"But this is the most serious threat." If he told her about the paper trail, he would have to explain how he got it. But that was a last resort. If he couldn't convince her to accept his help any other way, he would tell her what he could about the work he did outside the music industry.

"You seem to know a lot about what's going on in my life."

She studied him with deep brown eyes that still had the power to draw him in and lure him past reason.

"I told you, Celia. I care enough to keep tabs. I care enough to want to make sure you're okay."

"Thank you. That's…nice." Her braced shoulders eased, some of her defensiveness draining away, as well. "I appreciate your concern, even if it's a little confusing. I will be careful. Now that you've fulfilled your sense of…obligation or whatever, I truly do need to pack up and go home."

"I'll walk you to your car." He raised a hand and plastered on his best smile. "Don't bother saying no. I can carry your books, like old times."

"Except for your whole secret-service-style protective detail."

"You'll be safe with me." More than she could know.

"That's what we thought eighteen years ago." She stopped and pressed a hand to her forehead. "I'm sorry. That wasn't fair of me."

His mind exploded with images of their teenage passion, out-of-control hormones that had led them to reckless sex. A lot of sex. He cleared his throat. Too bad his brain still hitched on the past.

"Apology not needed but accepted." He knew he'd let her down then, and damned if he would repeat the mistake. "Let me take you out to dinner, and we can talk over an idea I have for making sure you're safe until the trial's over."

"Thank you, but no." She closed the laptop on her desk and tucked it in a case. "I have end-of-the-year grades to finish."

"You have to eat."

"And I will. I have half of a leftover panino waiting in my refrigerator at home."

She might be a more poised woman now, but there was no missing the old Celia stubbornness. She'd dug in her heels, and it would take serious maneuvering to budge her.

"Fine, then you leave me no choice. I'll talk now. This threat against your life is real. Very real. In my line of work—" his real line of work, which only a handful of people knew about "—I have access to security sources you can't imagine. You need protection beyond anything the local police department can provide and more than your father can buy."

"You're being overly dramatic."

"Drug lords, Celia, have unlimited funds and no scruples." He'd taken the fall for those types as a teenager to keep his mother safe. And it was his own fault for putting himself in their path by working in that club as a last-ditch effort to make enough money to support Celia and their baby on the way. "They will hurt you, badly, even kill you, in hopes of swaying your father."

"Do you think I don't already know this?" Her jaw flexed as she clenched her teeth, the only slip in her carefully controlled composure. "I've done everything I can."

He saw his opening and took it. "Not everything."

"Fine, Mr. Know-It-All," she said with a sigh, sweeping back her silky hair from her face. "What else can I do?"

Clasping her arms, he stepped closer, willing himself not to cave to the temptation to gather her soft body close against him and kiss her until she was too dizzy to disagree. Although if he had to use passion to persuade her, then so be it. Because one way or another, he would convince her. "Let my bodyguards protect you. Come with me on my European tour."

Two

Go on a European tour? With Malcolm?

Celia grabbed the edge of her desk for balance and choked back her shock at his outlandish offer. He couldn't possibly be serious. Not after eighteen years apart, with only a few short letters and a couple of phone calls exchanged in the beginning. They'd broken up, drifted away from each other, eventually cut off contact completely after the baby's adoption was complete.

Back at the start of Malcolm's music career, she'd been in her early twenties, under the care of a good therapist and going to college. She'd dreamed of what it would be like if Malcolm showed up on her doorstep. What if he swept her off her feet and they picked up where they'd left off?

But those fantasies never came to fruition. They only held her back, and she'd learned to make her own realities—concrete and reasonable plans for the future.

Even if he *had* shown up before, she wasn't sure then or now if she would have gone with him. Her mental health had been a hard-won battle. It could have been risky, in her fragile state, to trade stability for the upheaval of a life on the road with a high-profile music star.

But it sure would have been nice to have the choice, for him to have cared enough to come back and offer. His ridiculous request now was too little, too late.

Celia hitched her floral computer bag over her shoulder and eyed her office door a few short steps away. "Joke's over, Malcolm. Of course I'm not going to Europe with you. Thanks for the laugh, though. I'm heading home now rather than stick around through my planning period since, for the first day in forever, I'm not slated for bus duty. You may have time to waste playing games, but I have grades to tabulate."

His hand fell to rest on her bare arm, stopping her. "I'm completely serious."

Hair prickled. Goose bumps rose. And damn it, desire stirred in her belly.

After all this time, her body still reacted to his touch, and she resented the hell out of that fact. "You're never serious. Just ask the tabloid reporters. They fill articles with tales of your charm on and off camera."

He angled closer, his grip firm, stoking long-buried embers. "When it comes to you, I've always been one hundred percent serious."

And wasn't that an about-face for them? She used to be the wild, adventurous one while Malcolm worked hard to secure his future. Or at least, she'd thought he'd been serious about the future—until he'd ended up in handcuffs, arrested.

Her breath hitched in her throat for three heavy heartbeats before she regained her equilibrium. "Then I'll be the rational one here. There's truly no way I'm leaving for Europe with you. Thank you again for the offer to protect me, but you're off the hook."

He tipped his head to the side, his face so close a puff of her breath would rustle the stubborn lock of hair that fell over his forehead. "You used to fantasize about making love in Paris in the shadow of the Eiffel Tower." His voice went husky and seductive, those million-dollar vocal cords stroking her as effectively as any glide of his fingers.

She moved his hand slowly—and deliberately—off her arm. "Now I'm *really* not going anywhere with you."

"Fine. I'll cancel my concert tour and become your shadow until we're sure you're safe." He grinned unrepentantly, stuffing his hands in his pockets. "But my fans will be so pissed. They can get rabid sometimes, dangerous even, and above all, my goal is to keep you safe."

Was he for real?

"This is too bizarre." She clenched her fists to resist the urge to pull her hair—or his. "How did you say you found out about the Martin case?"

He hesitated for the barest instant before answering, "I have contacts."

"Money can buy anything." She couldn't help but think of how he'd once disdained her father's portfolio and now he could buy her dad out more than twice over.

"Extra cash would have bought us both some help eighteen years ago."

And just that fast, their final fight came rolling back over her, how he'd insisted on playing the gig at that seedy music joint because it paid well. He'd been determined for them to get married and be a family. She'd been equally as certain they were both too young to make that happen.

He'd gotten arrested in a drug raid on the bar, and she'd been sent to a Swiss "boarding school" to have her baby.

Even now, she saw the regret in his eyes, mixed with censure. She couldn't go down this path with him, not again. Tears of rage and pain and loss welled inside her, and while she understood how unhealthy it was to bottle her emotions, she refused to crumble in front of him.

She needed to get out of there before she lost it altogether and succumbed to the temptation to throw herself into the comfort of his arms, to bury her face in his shirt.

To inhale the scent of him until it filled her senses.

"Things would have turned out better for you with more financial options," Celia said, reminded of how he'd lost out on the promise of a scholarship to Juilliard. "But no amount of money would have changed the choices I made. What we shared is in the past." Securing her computer tote bag on her shoulder, she pushed past him. "Thank you for worrying about me, but we're done here. Goodbye, Malcolm."

She rushed by, her foot knocking and jangling a box of tambourines on her way out into the gymnasium. Malcolm could stay or go, but he wasn't her concern anymore. The custodian would lock her office after he swept up. She had to get away from Malcolm before she made a fool of herself over him.

Again.

Her sandals slapped an even but fast pace through the exit and directly into the teachers' parking lot. Thank heavens she didn't have to march through the halls with the whole school watching and whispering. Tears burning her eyes, she registered the sound of his footsteps behind her, but she kept moving out into the muggy afternoon.

The parking lot was all but empty, another hour still left in the school day. In the distance, the playground hummed with the cheers of happy children. What a double-edged sword it was working here, a job she loved but with constant reminders of what she'd given up.

Her head fell back, and she blinked hard. The sunshine blinded her, making her eyes water all the more. Damn Malcolm Douglas for coming into her life again and damn her own foolish attraction to him that hadn't dimmed one bit. She swiped away the tears and charged ahead to her little green sedan. Heat steamed up from the asphalt. Magnolia-scented wind rustled the trees and rolled across the parking lot. A flyer flapped under the windshield wiper.

She stopped in her tracks, her hand flying to her throat. Was that *another* veiled warning from her father's latest enemy?

Every day for a week, she'd found a flyer under her wiper, all relating to death. A funeral parlor. Cemetery plots. Life insurance. The police had called it a coincidence.

She pinched the paper out from under the blade, shuffling her computer bag higher up onto her shoulder. The flyer advertised…

A coupon for flowers? A sigh of relief shuddered through her.

An absolutely benign piece of paper. She laughed, crumpling the ad in her hand. She was actually getting paranoid, which meant whoever was trying to scare her had won. She fished out her keys and thumbed the unlock button on the key fob. Then she reached to slide her computer bag onto the passenger seat…

And stopped short.

A black rose rested precisely in the cup holder. There was no mistaking the ominous message. Somehow that macabre rosebud had gotten into her car. Some*one* had been in her locked vehicle.

Bile rose in her throat. Her mind raced back to the florist ad under her windshield wiper. She pulled the paper out of her computer bag and flattened the coupon on the seat.

Panic snapped through her veins, her emotions already on edge from the unexpected encounter with Malcolm. She bolted out of her sedan, stumbling as she backed away. Her body slammed into someone. A hard male chest. She stifled a scream and spun fast to find Malcolm standing behind her.

He cupped the back of her head. "What's wrong?"

With his fingers in her hair and her nerves in shambles, she couldn't even pretend to be composed. "There's a black rose in my car—completely creepy. I don't know how it got there since I locked up this morning. I know I did, because I had to use my key fob to get in."

"We call the cops, now."

She shook her head, nudging his hand aside. "The police chief will write it up and say I'm paranoid about some disgruntled students."

The old chief would make veiled references to mental instability in her past, something her father had tried to keep under wraps. Few knew. Still, for them, a stigma lingered. Unfair—not to mention dangerous since she wasn't being taken seriously.

From the thunderclouds gathering in Malcolm's eyes, he was definitely taking her seriously. He clasped her shoulders in broad, warm hands, gently urging her to the side and into the long shadows of his bodyguards. Malcolm strode past her to the sedan, looking first at the rose, then kneeling to peer under the car.

For a bomb or something?

She swallowed hard, stepping back. "Malcolm, let's just call the police after all. Please, get away from my car."

Standing, he faced her again, casting a tall and broad-shouldered shadow over her in a phantom caress. "We're in agreement on that." He charged forward and clasped her arm, the calluses on his fingers rasping against her skin. "Let's go."

"Did you see something under there?"

"No, but I haven't looked under the hood. I'm getting you out of here while my men make sure it's safe before the rest of the school comes pouring out."

The rest of the school? The sound of the children playing ball in the distance struck fear in her gut. The faces of her teacher friends and students scrolled through her head. To put an entire school in harm's way? She couldn't fathom whoever was threatening her would risk drawing this much attention—would risk this many lives. But there was definitely something more sinister about this latest threat, and that rattled her.

Malcolm tugged her farther from the vehicle.

"Where are we going?" She looked back over her shoulder at the redbrick building with the flags flapping in the wind. "I need to warn everyone."

"My bodyguards are already taking care of that," he reassured her. "We're going to my limo. It has reinforced windows and an armor-plated body. We can talk there and figure out your next move."

Reinforced windows? Armor plating? Security in front and behind? He truly did have all the money he'd once dreamed of, access to resources beyond her own local law enforcement. Enough resources to protect her from all threats, real or imagined.

She shivered in apprehension and didn't bother denying herself the comforting protection of Malcolm's presence all the way to his stretch Cadillac.

Malcolm stopped seeing red once he had Celia tucked into the safety of his armored limousine and the chauffer was headed for her home.

Two of his bodyguards had stayed with her vehicle to wait for the police—and report the details back to him without the filter of local authorities. He didn't think there was anything else wrong with her vehicle, but better to be certain and put all of his financial resources to work. He'd done all he could for now to make sure Celia and the school weren't in danger.

He scrolled through messages on his cell phone for updates from his security detail, all too aware of the warm presence of Celia in the seat beside him. Once he had her safely settled, he would work with his contacts to find substantial proof to nail that drug-dealing bastard Martin for these threats. Malcolm had taken the fall for a drug-dealing scumbag in return for them leaving his mother alone. He hadn't known who to turn to then.

He wasn't a flat-broke teenager anymore. He had the resources and power to be there for Celia now in a way he hadn't before. Maybe then he could finally forgive himself for letting her down.

As they drove down the azalea-lined Main Street, he felt the weight of her glare.

Malcolm tucked away his phone and gave her his undivided attention. "What's wrong?"

"Something that just occurred to me. Did you put that flower in my car to scare me so I would come with you?" She stared at him suspiciously.

"You can't possibly believe that."

"I don't know what I believe right now. I haven't seen

you in nearly two decades. And the day you show up, offering to protect me, *this* happens. The thought that they
were here, at the school, near my students..." Gasping for
air, she grabbed her knees and leaned forward. "I think
I'm going to be sick."

He palmed between her shoulder blades, holding himself back from the urge to gather her close, just to touch
her again. "You know me. You know how much I wanted
to take care of you before. You of all people know how
much it frustrated me that my dad wasn't there to take
care of my mom. Now, ask me again if I put the rose in
your car?"

Sweeping her hair aside with her hands, she eyed him,
her breath still shallow. "Okay, I believe you, and I'm
sorry. Although a part of me wishes you had done it because then I wouldn't have to be this worried."

"It's going to be all right. Anyone coming after you
will have to get through me," he said, tamping down the
frustration of his teenage years when there hadn't been
a damn thing he could do for Celia or his mom. Times
were different now. His bank balance was definitely different. "The police are going to look over your car and
secure the parking lot if there's a problem."

"Ten minutes ago you said the police can't protect me."

Dark brown locks slithered over his arm, every bit as
soft as he remembered. He eased his hand away while he
still could. He might not believe in the power of love anymore, but he sure as hell respected the power of lust. His
body still reacted to her, but this wasn't just any woman
who'd caught his eye. This was Celia. The power of the
attraction—as strong as ever—had caught him unawares.
But he'd come here to make up for the past. What they'd
shared was over. "We still need to let the police know.
Where is your father? At the courthouse?"

"At his annual doctor's checkup. His heart has been giving him trouble. He's been talking about retiring after the Martin case." She sagged back into the leather seat. "I can't believe this is happening."

He opened the mini-fridge and pulled out a bottled water. "No one will get to you now." He passed her the cooled Evian. "This vehicle is steel-reinforced, with bulletproof glass."

"Paparazzi can be persistent." She took the bottle from him, taking special care to avoid brushing his fingers. "Is it worth it living in a bubble?"

"I'm doing exactly what I want with my life." He had a freedom now that went far beyond the musician lifestyle, a side to his world with power that only a handful of people knew about.

"Then I'm happy for you." She sipped the water, all signs of her fear walled away.

But he knew what he'd seen, even if she was far better at hiding her emotions now than she'd been as a teenager. "Your school year finishes tomorrow. You'll be free for the summer. Come with me to Europe. Do it for your dad or your students, but don't let pride keep you from accepting my proposal."

She rolled the bottle between her hands, watching him from under the dark sweep of her eyelashes. "Wouldn't it be selfish of me to take you up on this offer? What if I put you in danger?"

Ah. He resisted the urge to smile. She hadn't said no. Something was shifting in her; he could sense it. She was actually considering his offer.

"The Celia I knew before wouldn't have worried about that. You would have just blasted ahead while we tackled the problem together."

A bump in the road jostled her against him. His arm

clamped around her instinctively, and just as fast his senses went on overload. The praline scent of her. The feel of her soft breasts pressed against his side, her palm flattened on his chest. And God, what he wouldn't give for a taste of her as she stared up at him. Her wide brown eyes filled with the same electric awareness that snapped through his veins.

Biting her lip, she eased away, sliding to the far side of the seat. Away from him.

"We're all grown up, and a more measured approach is called for," she said primly, setting the water bottle into a holder. "I can't simply go to Europe with you. That's just…unthinkable. As for my students, you already noted the school year's over, and if the threat truly is stemming from my father's case, it should be resolved by the time summer's over. See? All logical. Thank you for the offer, though."

"Stop thanking me," he snapped, knowing too well the ways he'd come up short in taking care of her and their child. This was his chance to make up for that, damn it, and he couldn't let it pass him by.

The limo cruised down the familiar roads of Azalea with blessedly smaller potholes. Not much had changed; only a few of the mom-and-pop diners had folded into chain restaurants near a small mall.

Otherwise, this could have been a date of theirs years ago, driving around town in search of a spot to park and make out. They'd both lost their virginity in the back of the BMW she'd gotten for her sixteenth birthday. The memories… Damn… Too much to think about now while trying to keep his head clear.

When he'd come up with the plan to help her, he hadn't expected to still want her, to be so pulled in by her. He'd dated over the years and could have any woman he wanted. And still, here he was, aching to take *this* woman. Had he gotten himself in too deep with his offer of protection? The prospect of touring Europe together, staying alone in hotels, suddenly didn't sound like such a smart idea.

"Malcolm?" Her voice drew him back to the present. "Why did you look me up now? I truly don't believe you've watched my every move for nearly eighteen years."

Fair enough. He had kept track of her over the years. But this time of year, thoughts of their shared past weighed heavier on his conscience. "You've been on my mind this week. It's the time of year."

Celia's eyes shut briefly before she acknowledged, "Her birthday."

His throat closed, so he simply nodded.

Her face flooded with pain, the first deep and true emotion she'd shown since he arrived. "I am sorry."

"I signed the papers, too." He'd given up all custodial rights to his child. He'd known he had no choice, nothing to offer and no hope of offering her anything in the foreseeable future. He'd been lucky not to be in jail, but the military reform school in North Carolina had been a lockdown existence.

"But you didn't want to sign the papers." She touched his arm lightly, the careful poise in her eyes falling away to reveal a deep vulnerability. "I understand that."

His willpower stretched to the limit as he fought back the urge to kiss away the pain in her eyes.

"It would have been selfish of me to hold out when I had no future and no way to provide for either of you." He shifted in his seat and let the question roll out that had plagued him all these years. "Do you think about her?"

"Every day."

"And the two of us?" he pushed, studying her hand

still resting on his wrist. Her touch seared his skin with memories and, yes, a still-present desire to see if the flame between them burned as hot. "Do you think back and regret?"

"I regret that you were hurt."

He covered her hand with his and held tight. "Come with me to Europe. To stay safe. To ease stress for your old man. To put the past to rest. It's time. Let me help you the way I couldn't back then."

She nibbled her bottom lip and he sensed that victory was so damn close....

The limo eased to a stop in front of her home. She blinked fast and pulled her hand away. She gathered her computer bag from the floor. "I need to go home, to think. This is all too much, too fast."

She hadn't said an outright no, and that would have to do for now. He would win in the end. He always did these days. His fame and position had benefits.

He ducked out of the car and around to her side to walk her to her door. He didn't expect to come inside and stay the night, but he needed to be sure she was safe. His hand went to the small of her back by instinct as he guided her toward the little carriage house behind a columned mansion.

She glanced over her shoulder. "You already know where I live?"

"It's not a secret." In fact her life was too accessible. He'd seen too much corruption in the world. This kind of openness made him itchy.

Although he had to confess to being surprised at her choice for a home. The larger, brick mansion wasn't her father's house, as he'd half expected when he'd first learned of where she lived. She'd carved out her own space even if she'd stayed in her hometown.

Even so, the little white carriage house was a security nightmare. Dimly lit stairs on the outside led to the main entrance over her garage. He followed her up the steps, unable to keep his eyes off the gentle sway of her hips or the way the sunlight glinted on her silky dark hair.

She stopped at the small balcony outside her door, turning to face him. "Thank you for seeing me home and calling the cops. I truly do appreciate your help."

How many times had he kissed her good-night on her doorstep until her father started flicking the porch light off and on? More than he could count. A possessive urge to gather her close and test the old attraction seared his veins, but he was a more patient man these days. He had his eye on the larger goal.

Getting her to leave the country with him.

He held out his hand for her keys. "Once I've checked over your place, I'll be on my way for the night."

Just not far away.

Malcolm wasn't the same idealistic teen he'd once been. He'd spent every day at that military reform school plotting how he would show up at Celia's father's house. How he would prove he hadn't done a damn thing wrong. He was an honorable man who'd had his family stolen from him. He'd held on to that goal all through college, as well, playing music gigs at night to earn enough money to cover what scholarships didn't.

But he never could have foreseen the path to honor that would play out for him. He'd sure as hell never planned on being a music star with his face plastered on posters. He'd stuck with it for the money. Then surprisingly, his old headmaster had shown up in his dressing room after a concert with a crazy offer.

Malcolm's globe-trotting lifestyle offered him the perfect cover to work as a freelance agent for Interpol.

In that moment, Malcolm gained a strong compass for his life and he'd never veered from the plan. Until today.

Even after eighteen years, he couldn't look away from Celia. "The keys, please?"

Hesitating for an instant, she dropped the keys into his hand. He turned the lock—a lock he could have picked thanks to some skills he'd acquired along the way—and pushed open the door to an airy and light space with sheer frills, an antique upright piano and a lemony, clean scent.

He stepped inside to make sure there weren't any more roses—or worse—waiting for her. She disarmed the alarm, then walked beside him down the narrow hall leading toward the living area, clicking her fingernails along a panpipe hung on the wall. His sixth sense hummed on high alert. Something wasn't right, but his instincts were dulled around Celia, and damn it, that wasn't acceptable. He knew better. He'd been trained for better.

Drawing in his focus, he realized… Holy hell…

He angled back to Celia. "Did you leave the living room light on?"

Flinching, she gasped. "No. I never do…"

He tucked her behind him only to realize…a man sat on the sofa.

Her father.

Malcolm resisted the urge to step back in surprise. Judge Patel had gotten old. Intellectually, Malcolm understood the years had to have left a mark, but seeing that in person was…unsettling. He'd resented this man, even hated him at some points, but bottom line, he understood they both had a common goal: keeping Celia safe.

Malcolm was just better suited for the job, and this time, he refused to let Judge George Patel stop him.

Three

Celia could swear she heard Fate chiming with laughter.

She looked from her father to Malcolm, waiting for the explosion. They'd never gotten along. Malcolm encouraged her to think for herself. Her parents had pampered her while also being overprotective. They'd seen her relationship with Malcolm as dangerous. They'd been right, in a way. She had been out of control when it came to him.

However, their refusal to let her see him had only made her try all the harder to be with him. Malcolm had chafed at their disapproval, determined to prove himself. The whole thing had been an emotional train wreck in the works.

Could they all be more mature now? God, she hoped so. The thought of an ugly confrontation made her ill, especially at the tail end of a day that had already knocked her off balance in more ways than one.

Malcolm nodded to her father. "Good evening, sir."

"Douglas." Her father stood, extending his hand. "Welcome back."

They shook hands, something she wouldn't have believed possible eighteen years ago. Even if they were eyeing each other warily, they were keeping things civil. The last time they'd all been together, her father had punched Malcolm in the jaw over the pregnancy news, while her mother had sobbed on the couch. Malcolm hadn't fought back, even though he was at least six inches taller than her father.

Nervous about pushing their luck, she turned to Malcolm and rested her fingers lightly on his arm. "I'm fine now. You can go, but thanks again, truly."

She shuddered to think what it would have been like to find that macabre rose on her own and have her concerns discounted by the police again. This was not the work of some student pissed off over a failing grade. Malcolm seemed to grasp that right away. She hadn't considered until just this moment how much his unconditional belief meant to her.

He dipped his head and said softly, "We'll talk tomorrow. But don't say no just because I'm the one offering." Grasping the doorknob, he nodded to her father again. "Good night, sir."

And that was it? He actually left? No confrontation? Celia stood there stunned at how easily he'd departed. She wanted a proper goodbye, and it scared her how much that mattered. Although his final words swirled in her mind. Was she being contrary—like the old Celia—turning down a wise opportunity because Malcolm had made the offer?

She shook off the thoughts. Likely Malcolm just realized she was safely home, his duty done. After resetting the alarm, she turned back to face her dad. The familiarity of her place wrapped around her, soothing her at the end of a tumultuous day.

This little carriage house wasn't as grand as the historic mansion where she'd grown up or the posh resorts Malcolm frequented—according to the tabloids. But she was proud of it. She took pride in how she'd decorated on her own budget. She'd scoured estate sales and flea markets until she pieced together a home that reflected her love of antiques and music.

Her home had become a symbol of the way she'd pieced herself back together, reshaping herself by blending the best of her past and her future. Shedding the dregs, taking responsibility for her own messes, which also gave her the freedom to celebrate her own successes.

And in finding that freedom, being around her father had actually become easier. She wasn't as defensive, and right now, she was only worried—about him.

"What are you doing here, Dad? I thought you were at your doctor's appointment."

"News travels fast." He nudged aside throw pillows and sank back on the couch, looking weary with bags under his eyes and furrows in his brow. "When I heard about Malcolm Douglas's impromptu visit to the school, I told the doc to speed things along."

His shock of gray hair still caught her by surprise sometimes. Much like when she'd been stunned to realize her indomitable father was actually only five-six. He'd always had a larger-than-life presence. Yet the day her mother had died, her father had grown frail in an instant, looking more and more like Grandpa Patel—without the Indian accent.

Intellectually, she'd always understood that her mom and dad were older than her friends' parents. She'd been a late-in-life baby, born after her sister died. How strange to have a sibling she'd never met.

And yes, more than once, Celia had wondered if she would have been conceived had her sister lived.

She'd never doubted her parents' love or felt she was a replacement for the child they'd lost to cancer. But that loss had made them overprotective, and they'd spoiled her shamelessly. So much so that Celia winced now to think of what a brat she'd been, how many people she'd hurt.

Including Malcolm.

She glanced at her slim silver watch. "He showed up at school less than an hour ago. You must have rushed right over."

"As I said, small town."

There weren't many secrets around Azalea, Mississippi, which made it all the more miraculous that she'd managed to have a baby and give her up for adoption without the entire town knowing all the details. Malcolm had been sent off to a military reform school in North Carolina, and she'd been sent to Switzerland on an "exchange" program, actually a chalet where she'd been homeschooled until she delivered.

She swallowed the lump in her throat and sat on the arm of the sofa. "What did the doctor say about your shortness of breath lately?"

"I'm here, aren't I? Doc Graham wouldn't have let me leave unless she thought I was okay, so all's fine." He nudged his round steel glasses in place, ink stains on his fingers from making notes. Her dad didn't trust computers and backed everything up the old-fashioned way—on paper. "I'm more worried about you and your concerns that someone might be targeting you."

Her concerns? Did he doubt her, too? "How bad is the Martin case?"

"You know I can't talk about that."

"But it's an important one."

"Every judge dreams of leaving the bench with a land-mark case, especially just before he retires." He patted the top of her hand. "Now, quit trying to distract me. Why did Malcolm Douglas show up here?"

"He heard about the current case on your docket, and somehow word got out about my reporting the threats to the police, which I find strange since no one here takes them seriously." Would they finally listen to her after today's incident?

"And Malcolm Douglas—international music star— came running after not seeing you for eighteen years?" Concern moved through his chocolate-brown eyes.

"Seems crazy, I know." She toed a footstool made of an old leather drum. "Honestly, though, I think it had more to do with the timing."

"Timing of what?"

That he even had to ask hurt her heart. "Dad, it's her seventeenth birthday."

"You still think about her?"

"Of course I do."

"But you don't talk about her."

She'd done nothing *but* talk about her baby in ther-apy—cry and talk more, until finally she'd reached a point where she could move forward with her life. "What's the point? Listen, Dad, I'm fine. Really. I have end-of-the-year grades to tabulate and submit."

Her dad thumped his knees. "You should move home."

"This is my home now," she reminded him gently. "I consented to letting you pay for a better security system. It's the same one at your house, as you clearly know since you chose the pass code. Now, please, go home and rest."

She worried about him, about the pale tinge to his

dusky complexion, the tired stoop to his shoulders. His job would be easier if she wasn't around since he wouldn't have to stress about her. Not taking Malcolm up on his offer suddenly felt very selfish. "Dad, I'm thinking about taking a vacation, just getting away once school ends."

"If you come to the house, you'll be waited on hand and foot." He continued to offer, and she continued to say no, a pact she'd made with herself the day she'd graduated from college at twenty-four. It had taken her an extra two years, but she'd gotten there, by God.

"I have something to tell you, and I don't want you to misunderstand or be upset."

"Well, you'd better spit it out, because just saying that jacked my blood pressure a few points."

She drew in a deep breath of fortifying air before saying quickly, "Malcolm thinks I should go on tour with him."

His gray eyebrows shot upward, and he pulled off his glasses and cleaned them with a handkerchief. "Did he offer because of the reports made to the police?"

She weighed whether or not to tell him about the incident with the rose, but then given how fast he'd heard about Malcolm's arrival, he would hear about the little "gift" in her car soon enough. "There was another threat today."

He stopped cleaning his glasses abruptly, then slid them slowly on again. "What happened?"

"A cheesy black rose left in my car." As well as the florist coupon in some kind of mocking salute. She tried to downplay the whole thing for her father, but her voice shook and she probably wasn't fooling him in the least. Still, she plowed ahead, trying her best to put his mind at ease. "Next thing you know, they'll be leaving a dead horse somewhere like a parody of *The Godfather*."

"This isn't funny. You *have* to move back home."

Seeing the vein at his temple throb made her realize all the more how her being around right now made things more difficult for him. "Malcolm offered the protection of his own security people. I guess crazed stalker fans rank up there with hired hit men."

"That's not funny, either."

"I know." And it wasn't. "I'm concerned he has a point. I make you vulnerable, and I placed my students at risk by waiting this long. If I go on his European tour, it will solve a lot of problems."

She didn't want her father to worry, but she had to admit there was something more to this decision than just her father. Malcolm had presented more than an offer of protection. He'd presented the chance to put their past to rest. Because he was right. The fact that she'd turned him down so promptly hinted at unresolved issues.

But could they really spend the whole tour together? A tour that lasted four weeks? She knew because, damn it, she periodically did internet searches on his life, wondering if maybe he would play at a local arena. He never did.

"That's the only reason you've made this decision?"

She hadn't decided yet. Or had she? "Are you asking me if I still have feelings for him?"

"Do you?" he asked and strangely didn't sound upset.

God, as if she wasn't already confused enough.

"I haven't spoken to him in years." Malcolm hadn't spoken to her, either, not since after the baby was born, and yes, that stung. "Aren't you going to push me again to come to your house?"

"Actually, no. Go to Europe." He studied her with those wise judge eyes. "Close that chapter on your life so you can quit living in limbo. I would like to see you settled before I die."

"I am settled," she said and then as an afterthought rushed to add, "and happy."

Sighing, her father stood, kissed her on top of the head. "You'll make the right decision."

"Dad—"

"Good night, Celia." He patted her arm as he walked past, snagging his suit jacket from the iron coatrack. "Set the alarm after I leave."

She followed him, stunned, certain she couldn't have heard what she thought she'd heard. Had her father really encouraged her to just pick up and travel around Europe with the former love of her life? A man reputed to have broken hearts around the globe?

Except, strangely, going to Europe with Malcolm was beginning to make sense. Going with him would solve her problems here, keeping her life ordered and safe. It was also her last chance to be with Malcolm, and the wild child she'd once been shouted for her go for it.

The newer, more logical side of her even answered that leaving with him would be the lesser of two evils.

Celia locked the door behind her father and keyed in the security code.

A noise from the hall made her jolt.

Her stomach gripped tight with fear and she spun around fast, grabbing a guitar propped against a chair and lifting it like a baseball bat. She reached for the alarm just as a large shape stepped out of her bedroom.

A man.

Malcolm.

He grinned. "Your security system sucks."

Malcolm watched the anger flush Celia's cheeks as her hand fell away from the alarm's keypad.

She placed the guitar on an armchair. "You scared the hell out of me."

"Sorry about that." He stepped deeper into her living room, a space decorated with antique musical instruments his fingers itched to try out. Later. First, he had business with Celia. "I thought I made it clear I'm worried about you being here alone."

"So you broke into my home?"

"Just to prove how crummy your security system is." He'd bypassed the alarm, climbed the nearby oak and made it inside her window in less than ten minutes. "Think about it. If someone like me—a plain ol' musician—could break into your place, then what about someone motivated to find you?"

"Your point has been made." She pointed to the door. "Now leave, please."

"But then you're still here, alone in the crappily secured apartment. My code of honor has trouble with that." He wandered lazily through her living room, inspecting the canvas over the fireplace, a sketch of band instruments and, below it on the mantel, an antique piccolo on a stand. "Gauging by your conversation with your dear old dad, you don't want to go to his place."

"You eavesdropped on my discussion with my father?"

"I did." He lifted the piccolo and blew into it, testing out a quick scale—not a bad sound for an instrument that appeared to be close to two hundred years old.

"You're shameless." She snatched the instrument from him and placed it back on the wall.

"I'm unrepentant, yes, and also concerned." He moved aside a brass music stand full of hand-scored songs— apparently for students, given her notes at the top—and sat on the piano bench in front of the old upright. "Since we're being honest, I heard it all, and even your father gave his consent for you to come with me."

"I don't need my dad's permission."

"Damn straight."

Watching him warily, she sat in a rocker by the piano. "You're trying to manipulate me."

"I'm trying to make sure you're safe—and yes…" He took her hand lightly in his. A benign enough touch. Right?

Wrong. The silkiness of her skin reminded him of times when he'd explored every inch of her. "Maybe we'll settle some old baggage along the way."

"This is too much."

He agreed. "Then don't decide tonight."

Her thick dark hair trailed over one shoulder. "We'll talk in the morning?"

"Over breakfast." He squeezed her hand once before letting go and standing. "Where are the sheets for the sofa?"

She gaped at him, smoothing her hands over wrinkles in her skirt. "You're inviting yourself to spend the night?"

He hadn't planned on it, but somehow the words had come out of him anyway, likely fueled by that reckless second when he'd touched her.

"Do you expect me to sleep on your porch?" He'd actually intended to sleep in the limo.

This was the man he was, the man he'd always been. He remembered what it was like for his mom living on her own. Call him old-fashioned, but he believed women should be protected. No way in hell could he just walk away. Especially not with images of the skirt of her dress hugging her soft legs.

"I would offer to get us a couple of rooms at a hotel or B and B, but we would have to drive for hours. People might see us. My manager likes it when I show up in the press. Me, though? I'm not as into the attention."

"Being seen at a hotel with you would be complicated." Her fingers twisted in the fabric she'd just smoothed seconds earlier.

"Very." He knelt in front of her, careful not to touch her just yet, not when every instinct inside him shouted to kiss her, to sweep her up into his arms and carry her to the bedroom. To make love to her until they both were too sated to argue or think about the past. He wasn't sure yet where he planned to go with those impulses. "So let me stay for dinner, and I'll bunk on your sofa. We won't talk about Europe tonight unless you bring it up."

"What does your girlfriend think of your being here?"

Girlfriend? Right now he couldn't even envision anyone except Celia. "Those damn tabloids again. I don't have a 'girlfriend.' My manager planted that story to make it look like I'm settling down."

Relationships were too messy, and more of that protective honor kept him from indulging in the groupies that flocked backstage. He "dated" women whose publicists lined up promo gigs with his publicist. As for sex, there had been women who kept things uncomplicated, women who needed anonymity and no strings as much as he did. Women as jaded about the notion of love.

"Is that why you're really here?" Her fingers kept toying nervously with the hem of her dress, inching it higher, revealing a tantalizing extra inch of leg. "You're between women and the timing fits?"

Something in her voice triggered warning bells in his mind. "Why is it so difficult to think I'm worried about you?"

"I just like my space. I enjoy the peace of being alone."

"So there's no guy in your life?" Damn it, where had that question come from?

A jealous corner of his brain.

She hesitated a second too long.

"Who?" And why the hell wasn't the man here watching out for her?

"I've just gone out with the high-school principal a couple of times."

The reports he'd gathered on her hadn't included that. His people had let him down.

"Is it serious?" he asked, her answer too damn important.

"No."

"Is it going to be?" He held up a hand. "I'm asking as an old friend." *Liar.* His eyes went back to her legs and the curve of her knees.

"Then you can ask without that jealous tone in your voice."

She always had been able to read him.

"Of course…" He winked. "And?"

She shrugged, absently smoothing the dress back in place again. "I don't know."

Exhaling hard, he rocked back on his heels. "I worked my ass off for that answer and that's all I get?"

"Pretty much." Hands on the arms of her chair, she pushed to her feet. "Okay. You win."

Standing, he asked, "Win what?"

"You can stay tonight—on the sofa."

He resisted the urge to pump his fist in victory. "I'm glad we're in agreement."

"You won't be so glad when you hear what's on the menu. I only have half a panino, barely enough for me. I was planning to shop once school finished."

"Dinner's on its way." He'd remembered about that

panino and had given his chauffeur instructions before he'd climbed the tree. He found the notion of an intimate dinner with Celia—discovering all the new secrets about her—stirring. "My very discreet driver will be delivering it."

"You already assumed I would agree? You're more arrogant than I recall."

"Thank you."

"That wasn't a compliment."

"That's all right." He soaked in the sight of her brown eyes flickering with awareness, her chest lifting faster with each breath. His hands ached to touch her, to relearn the curves, to find out if she still had the same sensitive areas and discover if she had new ones, as well. "It's for the best we don't exchange too many pleasantries."

She chewed the rest of the gloss off her bottom lip. "And why ever not?"

"Because honest to God," he growled softly, his body firing with a need that hadn't diminished one bit in nearly eighteen years apart, "I want to kiss you so damn badly it's already all I can do to keep my hands off you."

Four

Each seductive word out of Malcolm's mouth sent a thrill rippling through Celia. And not just his voice, but the strong lines of his handsome face, the breadth and power of his mature body—all *man*.

Teenage lust had ripened into a deeper, headier awareness. She still found him infinitely attractive, and the fact that she'd already been with him *many* times in the past only made that need edgier.

Dangerous.

Especially when they were only steps away from her bedroom.

She tipped her chin and steeled her will against temptation. "You used that line on me eighteen years ago. I would think your game would have improved since then. Or does being some kind of music legend make you lazy in the romance department?"

His head fell back, laughter rolling and rolling until he

scrubbed his hand over his face, grinning. "As I recall, my 'game' was just fine with you back then."

"Suffice it to say," she retorted, meeting his gaze with level strength, "my standards and expectations have changed."

"You want me to work harder." His eyes narrowed with the challenge.

"That's not what I meant." Her heart stuttered over a couple of beats before she found her balance and bravado again.

"What did you mean, then?" His hand grazed the keys of the upright piano, touching without stirring a note.

She shivered as she remembered the way he'd played so carefully over her skin long ago. "I was sixteen." She tapped out a quick tune on the other end of the keyboard, her nerves all too ready for an outlet. "Tough sell? I think not."

"My poor ego." He skimmed a scale.

"Sorry to have wounded you." She mirrored his notes. How many times had they done this?

"No, I mean it. You're good," he said without a trace of sarcasm. "It's nice to have someone who's real around me, someone I can trust."

"Am I supposed to cry for the poor little rich rock star?"

"Not at all." He slid onto the piano bench, his scale taking shape into a tune, the music relaxing and drawing her in at the same time.

Unable to resist, she sat down next to him and continued to twine her notes with his as easily as taking in air. "You know, one of the things that attracted me to you before was how you never seemed impressed by my father's wealth or influence."

"I respect your father—even if he did get me sent away

from you. Hell, if I had a daughter and—" His melody tangled. "Ah, crap. Okay, let me roll back that statement and reframe it."

"I know what you meant." Her hands fell to her lap, the piano going silent. "No parent would be happy about their sixteen-year-old having sex, much less reckless sex."

His face went dark with guilt, his hand gravitating to her face until he cupped her cheek. "I should have protected you better."

"We *both* should have been more responsible." She put her hand over his without thinking, her body going on autopilot around him as it always had, whether with touches or with music.

In less than a day, they'd fallen right back into the synchronicity they'd shared before, and God, that scared her spitless. She'd dated other men—slept with other men—but being with them never had this sense of ease. Already, she felt herself swaying toward him as his body leaned into hers.

Magnetic.

His hand still held her face, the calluses on his fingers familiar, a reminder of the countless hours he devoted to playing the guitar. Music hummed through her now, the sound of the two of them occupying the same space.

Her lips parted in anticipation—

The doorbell rang.

She jolted back as it rang again. How had she missed someone coming up outside?

Malcolm stood, his hand sliding away, then coming back to stroke her jaw once again. "That's dinner." He frowned. "And my phone."

He pulled his cell from his pocket.

"Supper?" she parroted, surprised she could even speak at all. She vaguely recalled him mentioning sending his driver/bodyguard for food. He had a whole staff at his disposal day and night, another reminder of how different their worlds were these days.

On his way to check the door, Malcolm said over his shoulder, "My chauffeur will set everything up while I take this call. All I need is a blanket and pillow for the sofa."

Before she could answer, he'd opened the door, waving his driver inside and stepping outside with his phone. Clearly, he didn't want her to hear his conversation. Which made her wonder a little about what he had to say.

And wonder a lot about *who* he said it to.

How the hell had he almost kissed her?

Malcolm gripped the wooden rails of Celia's small balcony landing just outside her front door. With ragged breaths, he drew in muggy night air as he listened to his driver setting up dinner inside. Bodyguards were stationed in the yard below and outside the brick-wall fence.

Malcolm's cell phone continued to buzz, and he knew he had to answer. And he would return the call—as soon as his heart rate settled back to normal.

He'd come here to make amends with Celia. To put his feelings of guilt to rest by helping her now like he couldn't before.

Where did sex factor into that?

It didn't. It hadn't. Until he'd seen her again.

These days he had control over his libido, enjoying healthy, safe relationships. He'd sure as hell never forgotten to put on a condom ever again. But he knew protecting Celia was about more than safe sex. That wouldn't keep either of them safe from the heartache of resurrecting something that was long done.

Plucking his phone from his pocket, he thumbed Redial and waited for Colonel John Salvatore to answer. His old headmaster from boarding school.

Now his Interpol handler. The man had traded in a uniform for a closet full of gray suits worn with a red tie.

"Salvatore here," his longtime mentor answered in clipped tones, gravelly from years of barking military orders.

"Calling you back, sir. Any word on Celia Patel's vehicle?"

"I checked the local department's report and they lifted prints, but with so many students in the school, there are dozens of different impressions."

His frustration ratcheted up. "And the security cameras?"

"Nothing concrete, but we did pinpoint the time the flyer was placed on the vehicle. We just couldn't see who did it. Kids were on lunch break, and a large group passed in front of the camera. Once they cleared, the flyer was under the wiper."

Malcolm scanned the street beyond the brick security wall, monitoring the lazy traffic for warning signs. "So whoever placed it there appears to be cognizant of the school's surveillance system."

"Apparently. One of my people is in between assignments and agreed to look into it."

"Thank you, sir."

Salvatore oversaw a group of freelance agents and field operatives, mostly comprised of former students. People who knew how to push the boundaries. Individuals with high-profile day jobs that allowed them to move in influential circles for gathering intelligence.

Except, today Malcolm needed Salvatore's help, and as much as he hated to ask anyone for anything, when it came to Celia…well, apparently he still had a weak spot. "I have a favor to ask."

"With what?" Salvatore answered without hesitation.

"I need an untraceable car and some ID delivered here tonight." A safeguard in place to escape with Celia in the morning, just in case his gut feeling played out. He'd learned to trust his gut.

"Not that I'm arguing, but just curious," Salvatore said drily. Nothing had gotten by the old guy when he'd been headmaster, either. "Why not have your personal detail take care of that? You've got a top-notch team."

In fact, some of them were former agents.

"This is too important." *Celia* was too important. "If it were just me, I could take care of myself. But with someone drawing a target on Celia's back…"

His fist thumped the railing, words choking on the dread in the back of his throat.

"Fair enough." The questions ended there. The two of them worked that tightly together with that kind of faith. "Whatever you need, it's yours."

"Thanks. I owe you." More than he could ever repay.

Colonel John Salvatore had become his father figure. The only real father figure he'd ever known, since his biological dad cut out on his family in the middle of the night, moving on to play his next honky-tonk gig. The bastard had sent a birthday card from the Florida Keys when Malcolm turned eleven. He never heard from him again.

"Malcolm," Salvatore continued, "I can put security in place for her here in the States so you can go ahead with your tour without worries."

"She's safer with me."

Salvatore's chuckle echoed over the line. "You don't

trust her to anyone else. Are you sure you trust yourself with her?"

God, he hated how easily Salvatore could read him.

"With all due respect, sir, the word games aren't necessary. I would do anything to keep her safe. Anything." His eyes scanned the small patio garden beside her carriage house with flowers blooming in splashes of purples and pinks. He recognized the lavender she used to love. His mother would have known the names of them all. Some were planted in the ground, others in pots. A fountain had been built into the stone wall, a wrought-iron chair and small table beside it. One chair. She sat there alone.

He didn't have any right to wonder about who she saw. But he couldn't deny he was glad she hadn't added a chair for her principal buddy yet.

Salvatore pressed, "What if I decide you're needed elsewhere?"

"Don't ask me to make the choice," he snapped.

"Apparently you've already decided."

"I have." Celia's safety would come first, even if it meant alienating Salvatore. Malcolm just hoped it wouldn't come to that. "Sir, I'm curious as to why the reports on Celia were incomplete."

"I don't know what you mean," he answered evasively.

"I respectfully disagree." Malcolm held his temper in check. Barely. "You're just trying to get me to say what I found out on my own in case I didn't learn everything. Then you can continue to hold back."

"We can play *this* game for a long time, Malcolm."

"Are you for or against me? Because I thought we were supposed to be on the same side."

"There are more people on your side than you know." When Malcolm kept his silence, Salvatore continued, "Celia's father did you a favor in getting you sent to my school. Without his intervention, you would have gone to a juvenile detention center."

Whoa. Hold on. He'd always thought the judge had pulled strings to get him out of Celia's life. The thought that her father had actually had a hand in helping Malcolm avoid jail time… He wasn't sure what to feel. He didn't want special favors. An important part of his life now consisted of helping to make people pay for their crimes.

After resenting Judge Patel for so long, this felt… strange. But then, because of his own dad, his gut made him naturally suspicious of other father figures. Which brought him right back around to the fact that Salvatore hadn't told him everything.

"What about this guy Celia's been seeing? The principal at the high school?"

"It didn't appear serious, so we didn't include it in the report. Apparently it *is* important to you, and that should tell you something."

"There are any number of ways that information could be important. What if he's the jealous type?" Um, crap, he could understand that too well. "Or if someone else is upset over the relationship. Details are important. Did you think I would go after him? You should know I'm not a headstrong idiot teenager anymore."

"You never were an idiot. Just young." Salvatore sighed, and Malcolm could envision the guy scratching a hand over his close-shorn salt-and-pepper hair. "I apologize for not including the principal in my report. If I find out anything else, I'll let you know. Meanwhile, whatever you need for protection, just ask and I'll make it happen."

Malcolm's temper inched down a degree. "Thank you, sir."

"Of course. Good night and be careful." The line disconnected.

Malcolm tucked his phone away but didn't go inside. Not yet. He couldn't avoid the truth staring him in the face. He'd just vowed he wasn't a headstrong idiot—yet he had acted like one in snapping at Salvatore, the man who had power and resources Malcolm needed. He'd all but proved the old man right, and all because he'd been knocked off balance by just the simple possibility of a kiss.

Except, nothing with Celia was simple.

It never had been.

His hands braced on the railing, he hung his head, staring down at that little garden grotto. He wanted to bring Celia down there and have a moonlit dinner together. The scent of those purple and pink flowers filled the air, while the music of the fountain filled the silence.

But he couldn't run the risk of someone seeing them. Not the bastard who'd been tormenting her. And not the press that hounded him.

Rather than regrets, he needed to focus on what he had. He had Celia to himself for the rest of the night. And by morning, he would have her rock-solid promise to come with him to Europe.

And he would keep his hands to himself.

Dinner together had been surprising.

Celia tucked the last of the dishes into the dishwasher while Malcolm checked the window for the umpteenth time. She'd expected him to press the issue of how close they'd come to kissing each other. She'd expected a big scene with oysters and wine and sexy almost-touches.

Instead he'd ordered shredded barbecue sandwiches that tasted like none she'd had before, served with Parmesan French fries and Southern sweet tea. There had even been pecan pie à la mode for dessert. The differences in their lifestyles didn't seem so big at moments like this.

She closed the dishwasher and pressed the start button. No busywork left to occupy herself, she had no choice but to face Malcolm—and the simmering awareness still humming inside her at the thought of kissing him again, touching him, taking things further. When they were teenagers, they'd spent hours exploring just how to make the other melt with desire.

Her face went hot at the memories.

"Thank you for ordering in dinner. That beat the dickens out of a warmed-over panino."

He turned away from the window, his deep blue eyes tracking her every move. "I hope you don't mind that I indulged myself in some selfish requests. I travel so much that I miss the tastes of home. Next meal, you choose. Anything you want, I'll make it happen."

Anything?

Best not to talk about exactly what she wanted right now. She'd already let her out-of-control attraction to him embarrass her once this evening.

"What a crazy concept to have whatever you want at your fingertips." She curled up in an overstuffed chair to make sure they weren't seated close on the sofa—or piano bench—again. "Are you one of those stars with strange, nitpicky requests, like wanting all the green M&M's picked out of the candy dish?"

"God, I hope not." He dropped back onto the piano bench, sitting an arm's reach away. "I like to think I'm still me, just with a helluva lot more money, so I get to call the shots in my life these days. Maybe I should take a Southern chef with me on tour."

She hugged a throw pillow. "You always did like pecan pie."

"And blackberry cobbler. God, I miss that, and flaky buttermilk biscuits."

"You must have picked up some new favorites from traveling the world." Even in his jeans with a torn knee, he still had a more polished look with his Ferragamo loafers and…just something undefinable that spoke of how much he'd accomplished. "You must have changed. Eighteen years is a long time."

"Of course I'm different in some ways. We all change. You're certainly not exactly the same."

"How so?" she asked warily.

"There. Just what you said now and how you said it." He leaned back against the piano. "You're more careful. More controlled."

"Why is caution a bad thing?" Her impulsive nature, her spoiled determination to have everything—to have him—at any cost had nearly wrecked both their lives.

"Not bad. Just different. Plus, you don't smile as much, and I've missed your laugh. You sound better than any music I've heard. I've tried to capture it in songs, but…" He shook his head. His blue eyes went darker with emotion, just the way they'd done all those years ago, and in that familiar moment, she felt his presence as deeply as she ever had from his kiss.

"That's so…sad." And incredibly touching.

One corner of his mouth kicked up in a wry smile. "Or sappy. But then, I make my living off writing and singing sappy love songs."

"Off of making women fall in love with you." She rolled her eyes, trying to make light of all the times the tabloid photos of him with other women had made her ache with what-ifs.

"Women aren't falling for me. It's all an image created by my manager. Everyone knows it's promo. None of it's real."

On a certain level, she got what he was saying, but something about his blasé attitude niggled at her. "You used to say the music was a part of you." She waved toward the antique upright behind him. "You were so passionate about your playing and your songs."

"I was an idealistic teenager. But I became a realist." He scooped up a stack of sheet music off the stand beside the piano. "I left this town determined to earn enough money to buy your father twice over, and music—" he rattled the pages in his hand "—was the only marketable skill I had."

"You achieved your financial goal. I truly am happy for you. Congratulations on succeeding in showing up my old man."

"More than succeeded." His eyes twinkled like stars lighting the night sky.

"So you can more than buy him out twice over. How many times over, five?"

He shrugged, his eyes still smiling.

Her jaw dropped. "Eight?"

He tossed the sheet music—scores she'd written for private students—back onto the side table.

"More than ten?" Holy crap.

"That's fairly close."

"Wow." She whistled softly. "Love songs pay well." A lot better than the little compositions she made for her students with dreams of putting them into an instruction book one day.

"People want to believe in the message," he said drily.

"You sound cynical." That made her sad when she thought of how deeply he'd cared about his music. "Why sing about something you don't accept as true? You obviously don't need the money anymore."

"You used to like it when I sang to you." He turned on the bench and placed his hands on the keyboard, his fingers starting a simple ballad, hauntingly familiar.

"I was one of those sappy women falling for you." When she'd been in Switzerland, his baby growing inside her, she'd dreamed of how they could repair their relationship when she got back and he finished his probation. Except, his letters to her grew fewer and fewer until she realized what everyone had told her was true. Theirs was just a high-school romance.

He tapped out another couple of bars of the melody line of one of the songs he'd written for her back when they'd dated. He'd said songs were all he had to offer her. This particular tune, one he'd called "Playing for Keeps," had always been her favorite. His fingers picked up speed, layering new intricacies into the simpler song he'd composed long ago. When he finished, the last note echoed in her tiny carriage house.

In her heart.

Her breath caught in her throat, her eyes stinging with tears that blurred the image of his broad shoulders as he sat at the piano. She ached with the urge to wrap her arms around him and rest her cheek on his back. She hurt from the lost dreams of what she'd let slip away. Apparently, he'd let a whole lot slip away from him, too. She didn't want to think about how cynical he'd grown.

Swallowing hard, she let herself dare to ask, "Was it real, what we felt then?"

He stayed silent, turned away from her for so long she thought he wouldn't answer. Finally, he shifted around again to face her. The raw emotion on his face squeezed at her heart.

A long sigh shuddered through him before he spoke. "Real enough that we went through a lot of pain for each other. Real enough that sitting here together isn't some easygoing reunion."

With that heavy sigh of his, she realized he'd suffered, too, more than she'd ever realized. Somehow, that made her feel less alone. Yes, they'd hurt each other, but maybe they could help each other, too. Maybe the time had come for a coda of sorts, to bring their song to an end.

"Malcolm, what's Europe going to be like if just sitting here together is this difficult?"

"So you've decided to come with me? No more maybes?"

She shoved to her feet and walked to him at the piano. "I think I have to."

"Because of the stalker?"

She cupped his handsome, beard-stubbled face in her hands. "Because it's time we put this to rest."

Before she could talk herself out of something she wanted—needed—more than air, Celia pressed her lips to his.

Five

Malcolm might not have planned on kissing Celia, but the second her mouth touched his, there wasn't a chance in hell he could pull away. She tasted like the sweet, syrupy insides of pecan pie and more—more than he remembered. Familiar and new all at once.

The tip of her tongue touched his, sending a bolt of desire straight through him until he went so hard at the thought of having her that he ached. His body surged with the need to take her, here, now. Because based on even this one kiss, he knew it would be even better for them than when they had been inexperienced, fumbling teens learning their way around…then learning the pleasure of drawing it out.

God, she was flipping his world upside down all over again.

Then the kiss was over before it barely started.

Celia touched her lips with a trembling hand, her

chewed nails hinting at how frayed her nerves had been lately. "Not the smartest thing I've ever done. I pride myself on being wiser these days."

No offers to make up the couch for him. Definitely no offer for him to come to her room. He hadn't expected otherwise…although a man could hope.

"We don't always want what's good for us."

"True enough. I got caught up in the memories from the music. The fact that you remembered the song from before… Well, I would have to be heartless not to be moved. Except, now reason has set in. If I follow through on that kiss, Europe is going to be very awkward—"

"Celia, it's okay. You don't need to explain or say anything more." He traced his thumb along her mouth. "I won't go psycho because you don't invite me into your bed after one kiss."

Still, his mind filled with the fantasy of tearing each other's clothes off, of carrying her over to the piano and sitting her on the keyboard, where he would step between her legs and bury himself deep inside this woman who'd always moved him in a way no other could.

Which had him wondering if perhaps they could indulge in more. If it was every bit as inevitable now as it had been eighteen years ago.

Indecision shifted in her dark brown eyes. Could she really be considering it? His pulse ratcheted up to never-before-tested speeds. Except, then she shook her head and turned away.

"I can't do this," she mumbled, backing away until his hand slid from her face. From the hall closet, she pulled out a stack of sheets and a pillow, then tugged a quilt from the back of the sofa. "Good night, Malcolm."

She thrust the linens against his chest and pivoted on her heels before he could say a word. No question, she was every bit as rattled as he was. Resisting the urge to go after her, he still allowed himself to savor watching the gentle sway of her hips as she left. His body throbbed in response, and he knew the feel of her would stay imprinted on him long after she closed her bedroom door.

Silence echoed after her, the scent of lavender wafting up from the sheets she'd given him. He hadn't slept on a sofa since his early days in the music industry, going to college on scholarship in the mornings, still half-asleep from playing late-night gigs. He'd gotten a degree in music with a minor in accounting because, by God, no manager was ever going to take advantage of his finances. He refused to be one of those musicians who made billions only to file for bankruptcy later. He knew what poverty was like and how it hurt the people around him—how he'd hurt the people around him because of his own dumb decisions.

He was in control these days.

Shrugging the tension out of his shoulders, he tossed aside the sheet and shook out the blanket. He stayed at five-star penthouse suites on a regular basis, but he'd never forgotten where he came from—and he damn well never would. The day a person got complacent was the day someone robbed them blind.

He refused to be caught flat-footed ever again. The lowest day of his life had been sitting in that police cell, arrested for drug possession. Wondering what Celia thought. Hating that he'd let his mother down.

The part that still stuck in his craw? For some twisted reason, his brush with the law made him all the more alluring to fans. The press had spun it into a "bad turned good" kind of story. He didn't want fans glorifying him or the things he'd done.

His mistakes were his own. He took responsibility for

his past. Atonement wasn't something to parade around for others to applaud. Receiving praise diminished the power of anything he might have done right.

Speaking of atonement…

He tugged the leather briefcase from beside the sofa. His driver had left the essentials. He pulled out his tablet computer to check for an update from Salvatore on Celia.

Because, with memories of that kiss still heating his blood, he sure as hell wasn't going to fall asleep anytime soon.

Celia kept her eyes closed even though she'd woken up at least ten minutes ago after a restless night's sleep. Her white-noise machine filled the room with the sound of soothing waves. She snuggled deeper under the covers, groggy and still so sexually strung tight her skin was oversensitive to the Egyptian cotton sheets. Just one kiss, and she was already burning up for Malcolm Douglas again.

The thought of facing him was mortifying—and a little scary. What if she walked out there, lost control and plastered herself all over him again?

Last night's kiss had rocked her to her toes. And the way Malcolm hadn't pressed her to hop right into bed together? That rattled her even more. But then, he hadn't pressured her as a teenager, either. She'd been the aggressor. She'd known him for years. They'd shared a music teacher, even performed at recitals together. But something had changed when they both came back from summer break, entering their sophomore year.

Her friend had gotten hot.

The other high-school girls had noticed, too. But she'd been determined. He was hers. No one had ever denied her anything, and she could see now how that had made her all the more determined to win him over. Her selfishness had played a part in how recklessly fast she'd pursued him.

She'd justified her actions by noting the interest in his eyes. Except, he'd insisted he didn't have the time or money for dating. He'd told her they couldn't be anything more than friends. She'd told him she didn't need fancy romancing. She just wanted him....

After they'd been dating for five months, she'd feared she was losing him. His mother had been filling out applications for scholarships for him to attend a special high school for the arts. Celia understood Terri Ann Douglas wanted the best for her son, but it seemed the push for him to attend school out of town had more to do with getting him away from Celia than obtaining a better music education.

Or at least that was how it had appeared in her self-centered teenage mind.

Already she'd felt as if she barely got to see him between his job and their music lessons and their eagle-eyed parents. Still, they'd stolen time alone together to make out, talk, dream—make out some more. Their make-out sessions had grown hotter, as hot as possible without going all the way.

She recalled every detail of that whole day, the day she'd lost her virginity. She remembered what she wore—pink jeans and a rock-band T-shirt. What she ate—cereal, an apple and not much else, because she wanted to keep fitting into those jeans.

Most of all, she remembered what it felt like stretched out on the backseat of her car with Malcolm, parked by the river at night. She'd already pitched her shirt and bra onto the floor, along with his shirt, too, because there was nothing like the feel of her breasts against his bare chest.

Her hand tunneled down his pants, and he was working the zipper on her pink jeans. They'd already learned how to give each other orgasms by stroking to take the edge off the gnawing need.

Except, that night she'd been selfish. Scared of losing him. And most of all, she'd been stupid.

They hadn't used a condom.

Although she'd still needed him to finish her with his hand afterward because it hadn't been anywhere near as earth-shattering as she'd expected. Not the first time.

But she hadn't gotten pregnant then, either. Which made them all the more reckless over the following weeks when Malcolm had been deliciously determined to figure out exactly how to bring her to that earth-shattering release while buried heart-deep inside her....

Celia snuggled deeper under the covers, cocooning herself in memories. The good—then the bad when everything had fallen apart. For years she'd told herself maybe he hadn't loved her as much as she'd loved him. That they'd only become a couple because she'd gone after him, and what red-blooded teenage boy said no to sex?

But last night, the way he'd played that song made her realize she'd only been trying to ease her guilt over how much she'd cost him, how much their breakup had hurt him, as well.

Now this new insight complicated the trip to Europe.

In the harsh light of the morning, leaving with him seemed like a reckless idea, and she didn't do "reckless" anymore. She'd left behind impulsiveness when she'd passed over her baby girl to parents who could give her all the things Celia couldn't. The pain of loss had pushed her over the edge.

She had to be smarter this time, to be careful for her

own sake, and for his. Just the thought of seeing him once she walked into the living room sent butterflies whirling in her stomach.

Damn it. He hadn't even been back in her life for twenty-four hours, and desire for him had flipped her world upside down. She hadn't helped matters with that impulsive kiss, brought on by nostalgia. She couldn't let sex cloud their judgment again. She wanted—she needed—her peaceful existence. To make that happen, she had to stay in control while facing her fears and guilt in order to move on with her life.

She flung aside the covers and clicked off her white-noise machine, the sound of waves ending abruptly, only to be replaced by a different buzz coming from outside. Frowning, she went to the window and parted the wood shutters.

Oh. My. God. Her breath caught in her throat. She stepped away fast.

Her lawn was absolutely packed.

Cars, media vans, even tents with clusters of people underneath filled her yard and beyond, overflowing onto the sidewalk. She slammed the shutters closed and locked them. Her home had been invaded, and she was damn certain it had nothing to do with her stalker.

Apparently, Malcolm had about a million of his own.

She snagged her cotton bathrobe from the foot of her bed. Sprinting for the door, she yanked on her robe and knotted the tie on her way to the living room.

Only to stop short again.

Malcolm was sprawled on the sofa wearing only his jeans, with the blanket twisted and draped over his waist. Her mouth dried up. The muscles she'd felt ripple beneath his shirt were all the more magnificent uncovered. Damn it all, why couldn't he have gone paunchy and bald? Or why couldn't he have at least become a totally arrogant jerk?

All right. He was a bit arrogant, but not at all a jerk. And the six-pack abs didn't show the least sign of paunch. His hair was so freakin' magnificent his fans named that signature lock of hair over the brow—calling it "The Malcolm." Men everywhere were letting their hair grow long over their foreheads because their girlfriends begged them to. Malcolm's fans.

His fans.

Damn. Not two minutes after vowing not to let the attraction derail her, she'd failed. She'd been so caught up in gawking at his naked chest that she'd forgotten about the sold-out audience on her lawn. Celia knelt by the sofa, her hand falling lightly on his shoulder.

His warm skin sent sparks shimmering through her.

She snatched back her hand. "Malcolm? Malcolm, you have to wake up now—"

He shot upright off the sofa. His arm whipped from under the blanket, a gun clasped in his hand and pointed at the ceiling.

A gun?

"Malcolm?" she squeaked. "Where did that come from?"

"It's mine, and it's registered. I keep it for protection, which seems appropriate given the threats against you. Probably a bit more daunting to an intruder than if I bash them over the head with a rolled-up music score." He placed the black weapon on the coffee table with a wry grin. "It's best you don't surprise me when I'm asleep."

"Do you get creepy fans waking you up often?" She rubbed her arms, suddenly chilled.

"When I first hit the charts, a fan managed to get past security into the house. But since then, no. That doesn't mean I'm letting down my guard, and my security detail is an impenetrable wall between me and overzealous fans."

"Then why sleep with the gun?"

"Because your life is too precious to trust to anyone else. I have to be sure."

Her heart squeezed in her chest, and it was all she could do not to caress his face, kiss him, claim that perfect mouth of his all over again.

Clearing her throat, she nodded to the living-room window covered with simple white shutters instead of curtains. "Check out the lawn."

His eyes narrowed, muscles along his chest bunching. He strode across the room and opened the shutters just a crack.

"Crap." He stepped to the side, out of the sight line. "Wish I could say I'm surprised, but I was afraid this might happen. I should have insisted we leave last night before they had time to rally."

Her misgivings churned again. "About leaving together for Europe. I'm…"

"Yeah, I agree." He snagged his button-down shirt off the back of the chair, tucking his feet back into his loafers. "We need to go right away."

She toyed with the tie of her bathrobe. "I'm not so sure about that."

He glanced up from buttoning his shirt. "We don't have a choice, thanks to the folks on the lawn with cameras."

"So you more than suspected this *might* happen?"

"I couldn't be certain." He tucked his tablet computer into a leather briefcase. "But I had to consider it and plan accordingly."

"What kind of plan?"

"A way for us to leave before it gets worse." He strapped his gun into a holster and stowed it in the briefcase, as well. "As soon as you get dressed."

"It can get worse than that? There's no more room on the lawn."

"There's always room," he said darkly. "Get dressed, and I'll pour some coffee into travel mugs. We'll have to eat on the road."

"What if I decide to stay here and let you leave on your own?" So much for her resolution to face her fears. *Chicken.*

He stood still. Waiting. Leaving her time to realize— she really didn't have a choice anymore. Once the press saw him leave, they would stay on her lawn until she walked out the door or until they somehow managed to break in. She needed to tuck her head and get out of here quickly.

"Right." She sighed. "I'm going with you. But why so soon? What about packing?"

"Arranged."

"Of course."

He could order anything now, thanks to his money and power. And at the moment, she wasn't in the position to turn that down. His guards had the crowd contained, but for how long?

"God, this is getting complicated." She scraped back her tangled hair in her hand. "I have an end-of-the-year concert tonight and grades to file."

Malcolm held a phone in his hand. "Tell me what you want, and I'll make it happen. I can have an army of guards around the entire school if that's what you need."

As much as it pained her, she knew there was only one solution. "That sounds frightening and dangerous. I'll call the high-school chorus teacher. She can conduct the concert if I send her the lineup, and I can file my grades online. Given the circus out there, I imagine the school will understand my decision to take a personal day."

He reached out a hand. "Celia, I'm so damn sorry about—"

"Uh, really, it's okay." The last thing she needed was his touch scrambling her thoughts again. "You were just trying to help."

Spinning on her heel, she raced back down the hall to her room. She yanked a sundress and sandals from her tiny closet before peeling off her pj's.

She couldn't help but wonder, if Malcolm suspected this kind of fan fallout, then why had he made such a public appearance? Had he been trying to force her to fall in line with his plan? If so, why? What did he have to gain from stepping in to protect her from the stalker?

None of this made sense.

She tugged out fresh underwear and didn't stop to think about why she bypassed simple white cotton for lemon-yellow lace. It shouldn't have mattered, and she shouldn't have noticed her choice.

But it did matter, and she had noticed. That made her angry with herself all over again. It had been tough enough tamping down her runaway attraction after a night spent dreaming about him and that dang kiss. Now she had the additional memory of chiseled abs and his formidable male chest etched in her brain.

She yanked on her clothes and jammed her feet into sandals while the scent of hazelnut drifted into the bedroom from her kitchen. She took a valuable thirty more seconds to brush her teeth and hair, before racing back into the living room, grabbing her floral tote bag along the way so she would have her wallet and computer. "I guess it's time to put your guards to work helping us run the gauntlet to your limo."

He passed her a travel mug of coffee. "We're not using the limo. We'll go down the inside stairs to the garage."

"My car is still at the school." She shrugged her bag over her shoulder, nerves singing freaking arias in her stomach at the thought of all those fans outside. "I really should give my dad a call. And damn it all, Malcolm, just because I'm going with you does not mean we will be sleeping together. You have to understand—"

"Celia, stop. It's okay. I hear you. Now hear me. I had a vehicle delivered last night in case we needed to make an escape—since the limo wouldn't fit in your garage. You can call your father and the other music teacher once we're on the road." He slipped his fingers down her arm in a shivery caress then clasped her hand. "Trust me. I will not let anyone—including myself—hurt you."

With a gentle tug, he guided her down the narrow enclosed staircase and opened the door to reveal...

A red Maserati.

Her jaw dropped and her feet grew roots. "Oh. Um, that's a, uh, nice car."

Sleek and sophisticated, not unlike the man beside her. The man she'd seen half-dressed this morning.

"Better yet, it's a *fast* car." He opened her door then sprinted around the front to the driver's side. He settled behind the wheel and reached into the glove compartment for a blue ball cap. "Are you ready?"

"Nope." Her fingers curled into the supple leather. All the better to prevent her from touching Malcolm. "I guess that doesn't matter, though."

"Sorry about that." He tugged on the cap, clicked the garage door opener and revved the finely tuned engine to life. She caught the scent of his aftershave in the close confines of the sports car.

Her stomach twittered at every growl of the engine. The garage door rumbled as it rolled up, revealing the clusters of people outside.

Somehow, her hand sought out his forearm and squeezed.

As he nosed out, fans pushed at the line of security guards, the high-pitched squeals and flashing bulbs piercing even the thick, tinted windows.

Only a slight flex of muscles along Malcolm's jaw showed any frustration on his part. This was, after all, everyday life to him now. And so totally alien to her.

The deeper they drove into the swarm of fans and paparazzi, the more and more she felt like Alice in Wonderland falling headfirst into the rabbit hole.

An hour later, Malcolm floored the Maserati on a deserted country road. The high-performance vehicle had given him the speed and maneuverability to dodge the paparazzi that had trailed him out of Celia's garage. Miles of empty farm fields rolled ahead of them, broken by the occasional sprawling oak or faded red barn.

Best of all, there was almost zero traffic. Tractors chewed up the land off to the side. So far, only two trucks had passed going the other direction. She'd made her calls to reassure her father and to detail the program requirements for the other music teacher.

Finally, he had Celia safely away and all to himself. He wasn't trusting the press not to find the distinctive car, so he had more change-ups planned. For now, he had a short window to be with Celia, alone on the open road. He needed to use this time wisely to help put her at ease around him again. If he expected to make a serious go at putting the past to rest, then she had to stop walking on eggshells all the time.

She'd showed signs of cold feet about coming to Europe with him when she'd seen the press and fans packing her lawn. Although, that paparazzi sit-in had also offered him the perfect excuse to whisk her away faster. Once he got her out of town and away from whoever was trying to scare the hell out of her, then he could...

What?

Somehow with that kiss, things had shifted between them. In spite of what she'd said about not sleeping together, the heat between them was still there, but matured. He'd spent most of the night thinking about her, wanting her. They were both adults. They both had settled into their lives and careers.

She hadn't been ready to see that attraction through to its conclusion last night. He could understand that. He meant it when he'd said he would not do anything to hurt her or abuse her trust. But he had to accept that the kiss changed everything. Though he'd meant to stay away, he now knew he couldn't leave this mission without having her one last time.

As for their past feelings for each other? Puppy love. The flowery notion of soul mates was a crock. Something created to sell music, movies and greeting cards. He was a more practical man these days. He and Celia could indulge in sex without risking their hearts.

Now he just needed to convince her.

He glanced over at Celia, his eyes drawn to the curve of her legs. Hell, he was even turned on by her cute feet with pink-painted toenails peeking out of her sandals.

Crap.

Focus on the road, idiot.

He downshifted around a curve on the two-lane highway. "I'm sorry to have made you miss out on the concert."

"I know you were just trying to help."

"Still, it sucks to lose something you've obviously worked hard on." He felt the weight of her stare and glanced over to find her forehead furrowed. "What?"

"Thank you for understanding how important this was to me—for not dismissing it. I know we're not a sold-out coliseum or a royal audience."

"Music isn't about the size or income of the audience."

She smiled for the first time since they'd left her home. "It's about touching the heart, the soul."

His grip tightened on the wheel as he thought of another time she'd said much the same thing. One night, he'd brought along his guitar to serenade her under the stars. He'd picked up fast food and a blanket and told himself someday he would give her better. Give her more. She'd quickly reassured him that money didn't matter to her, just the heart and the soul.

He should have listened to her. She hadn't wanted this kind of life then any more than now. Regardless of what she wanted, though, she did need him. At least for the moment.

Accelerating, he sped down the deserted two-lane road.

Celia smoothed the wrinkles from her gauzy dress. "That was quite an impressive getaway. I thought for sure someone would get hit or at the very least have their toes run over. But you got us out of there without anyone getting hurt. Where did you learn to drive like that?"

"Part of the job training." Except, it had more to do with his Interpol work than the music world, but he tried to stick to the truth as much as he could, as if that somehow made up for the huge lie of omission. But then it wasn't something he had leave to work into conversation. *Hey, I moonlight as a freelance agent for Interpol.*

She laughed lightly. "I must have missed the driving class in my music education."

"I have a friend who's a race-car driver." Another truth. "He gave me lessons."

"What friend is that?" She turned toward him, hitching her knee up so her whole body shifted.

For a second, his gaze drifted to the hem of her dress. The hint of skin the movement had exposed.

"Elliot Starc. We went to school together."

She gasped. "You went to school with Elliot Starc, the international race-car driver?"

"You know about Starc?" He stared at the road harder and told himself to keep his head on straight. "Most of the women I've met don't follow racing."

"Honey, this is the South, where people live and breathe NASCAR." Her soft drawl thickened a little as she laughed again. "Starc is, of course, more Formula One, but some of my father's friends take their racing interests further."

"Fair enough. So you've heard of Eric, then."

"There must have been a lot of lessons to get that good at maneuvering…the speed." She shook her head, her hair shifting over her shoulders. "I'm still dizzy."

He glanced at her sharply. "Are you okay? I didn't mean to scare you."

"You didn't. I'm all right." She laughed softly. "Goodness knows I got enough speeding tickets as a teenager. I'm a more sedate driver these days. I no longer expect Daddy to fix my tickets for me."

"A lot of time has passed."

"Yet you're here. *We're* here." The confusion in her voice reached out to him. But before he could figure out what the hell to say, she continued, "I just don't want you to get hurt protecting me."

"I'll be fine. I told you. I have this under control." Too bad he couldn't say the same about his resurrected feelings for Celia.

He was aware of her every movement beside him.

"Oh, right. Your plan." She straightened in her seat again. "Where are we going?"

To the one place he could be certain no one would find them. "To my mom's house."

Six

His mother's house?

Celia still couldn't wrap her brain around that nugget of information even a half hour after he'd spilled the beans. The press had reported in the past that he now supported his mother, declaring she deserved a life of luxury after all the sacrifices she'd made for him. But there were never any details about where Terri Ann Douglas had relocated after she'd left Azalea fourteen years ago.

Quite frankly, Celia hadn't been that interested in staying in touch with the woman who reminded her so deeply of all she'd lost. Terri Ann hadn't approved of Celia back then anyway, and with good reason. Celia was everything the woman had feared for her son—spoiled, selfish and more than willing to toss away her virginity if that tied Malcolm closer to her.

The thought of seeing Terri Ann again sent Celia's stomach into knots as they pulled up to a large scrolled gate covered by vines. Cameras moved ever so slightly, almost hidden in the foliage. Malcolm stopped by the security box and typed a code into the keypad. The gates swung wide, revealing a road that lead into…nothing but trees.

She couldn't see a house, and wouldn't be able to see people, even if they showed up. The security was… beyond crazy. As she began to grasp the depth of the protection here, she had to wonder, had he changed his mind about Europe and decided to stash her away here with his mother, where he'd obviously already lavished a good deal of effort to ensure privacy?

Disappointment gripped her, too much considering she'd been questioning the wisdom of going with him. But she couldn't deny a flickering wish deep inside her. Yes, her world had spun out of control since he'd returned, but she didn't want to step off the dizzying ride just yet. This was crazy and scary, out of character for the new, steadier path she'd chosen for herself.

Except, even if they didn't sleep together again— which they weren't going to do, she emphatically reminded herself—she finally had a chance for answers, for closure on her teenage years, a time in her life that had almost broken her. She didn't want to lose the opportunity.

"Malcolm, would you care to clue me in to what's going on?"

He drove the car deeper into the forest of towering oaks and pines, gravel crunching under the tires. "I needed to regain some control over the security. We're off the radar now, which gives us some breathing room."

Suddenly, he turned from the dusty path onto a paved road. The leafy branches parted to reveal—*oh, my God*—a compound.

A columned mansion was surrounded by every convenience from a pool to tennis courts. Even a pond sported a small dock with a gazebo picnic area by the shore.

The home was a magnificent getaway. But at the moment, it looked rather like a prison to her. "Do you plan for me to stay here instead?"

He looked at her quickly. "Not at all. We're still going to Europe. I told you my security would be taking care of you, and I meant that. We're simply leaving from here instead of from a public airport."

Too much relief zinged through her. Damn it, she was supposed to be gaining peace from this reunion, not wanting to spend more time with him. "Then I'm fuzzy on the details of how we're getting from this place to Europe. I don't see an airstrip."

He pointed in the distance.

A helicopter flew just over the treetops.

She shrank back in her seat even though she knew the tinted windows provided complete privacy. "The press found us already?"

"No, that's our ride." He put the Maserati in Park next to a large concrete pad.

A space large enough for that bird to land. Holy cow.

Her eyes stayed locked on the white helicopter flying closer, closer still, until it hovered. Roaring overhead, it landed a few feet away, blades stirring dust all around the car. "You're kidding."

"Nope. We'll fly in the chopper to another location, where we'll board a private jet and leave the country. Avoiding the press involves a lot more steps than going from point A to point B."

Wow, okay. He did have resources beyond anything she'd imagined. But...

"I thought you said we were visiting your mother."

"I said we were going to her house. She's not here."
He pulled his briefcase from behind his seat. "She's at
her vacation flat in London."

A vacation flat? "You're a good son. This amazing
house. A place in England, too."

"What I give her is easy compared to all she did for
me." His eyes went sober, pained even. "The house, the
apartment, they don't even put a dent in my account. She
worked two jobs just to put food on the table. She even
cleaned my piano teacher's house in exchange for lessons. Mom deserves a retirement. Now, are you ready?"

She was running out of time to say what had been
chewing at her gut since last night. "I don't want you to
think that kiss meant more than it did."

"What did it mean?"

"That I'm still attracted to you, as well, that we share
a very significant past. But that doesn't mean we have a
future or that we should act on the attraction." Because
honest to God, right now she wasn't sure how she would
walk away from him a second time if they got even closer.
They needed to use this trip together to talk through what
happened when they were teenagers, to have the conver-
sations they'd been denied because of immaturity—and
the fact that he'd been locked away in a military school
and she'd been sent to Switzerland. "It was more of a fare-
well to that past and a salute to friendship kind of kiss.
Didn't you write a song once about goodbye kisses?"

"Someone else wrote that one." He smiled cynically.
"My manager thought it would melt hearts."

"It melted hearts all the way to the top of the charts."
She'd turned the radio station dozens of times to keep
herself from crying over that damn song.

"Call me jaded—" he gripped the steering wheel so

tightly his knuckles went bloodless "—but sometimes I feel like I'm selling a flawed ideal to my fans."

"How can you deny there's love out there?" She turned toward him again, clenching her hands into fists to keep from reaching for him. "We felt it. I know we did. That song last night proved it. Even though it ended, what we had was real."

"Puppy love."

Her head snapped back, his words a splash of bitterly cold water. "Are you being a bastard on purpose?"

"Just helping you resist the urge to kiss me again." He reached across her and opened her door. "Our helicopter's waiting."

As her door swung wide, the biting wind blew grit and rocks inside the beautifully magnificent car, stinging her as tangibly as his angry words had. She grabbed her floral tote bag full of schoolwork and jumped out, slamming the door closed behind her. Helicopter blades whomp, whomp, whomped, slicing the air. Who traveled by helicopter besides the military and the country's president?

Apparently platinum-selling stars did.

He opened the door for her. "Sit up front."

Gingerly, she climbed inside the helicopter, the scent of leather and oil saturating the air as she settled in place. She eyed the empty copilot's seat, the thrill-seeking ways of her teenage years nowhere to be found. The thought of riding in a chopper—of actually going to Europe—made her chest grow tight. She forced herself to breathe in and out evenly, willing back the rising panic attack.

Damn it, she could do this—she had to do this. She would use this time to turn the page once and for all on the chapter of her life that included Malcolm Douglas.

She snapped her seat belt on and tugged it extra tight while glancing at the controls and the thin sides, the surrounding glass. Okay, so maybe she could do this in a different seat. She turned to ask the pilot if she could sit in back but he slid out before she could speak. He passed his headset to Malcolm and put Malcolm's ball cap on his head. The pilot sprinted toward the Maserati.

Malcolm slipped into the pilot's seat. He tugged on his headset and passed a second set to Celia. She pulled them on, her ears filling with chatter over the airwaves.

He leaned toward her. "If you want to speak privately, just tap this button."

And with that, he ran a check of the controls, his voice resonating in her ears as he called in to some tower for takeoff. How could the people on the other end of the radio not know they were speaking to Malcolm Douglas? His smooth baritone caressed her senses even when he just spoke, his voice utterly recognizable to her even without looking at him.

There was no denying he knew exactly what to do. "Um, Malcolm? Are you actually going to fly this—"

The helicopter lifted off. She bit down a yelp and grabbed her seat, terrified of touching something. It wasn't as if she was afraid to fly, but this was all happening so fast, with so little explanation. She looked out at the house growing smaller and smaller the higher they flew.

"I guess you really are flying the chopper. You have a license, right?"

"Yes, ma'am."

"You can't tell me Elliot Starc taught you to drive this, too."

"Not Elliot." He glanced at her and winked. "Private instructor."

She sagged back in her seat. "Of course. How could I not have known?"

Reservations about her decision were pointless now.

She was going to Europe with the man who'd stolen—and broken—her heart eighteen years ago.

Malcolm steered the helicopter through the sky.

He had to admit there were definite perks to having an unlimited bank account. He had the coolest toys. His work with Interpol had only expanded the scope.

Plowing through the sky in a helicopter, having the little bird at his disposal, beat the hell out of the days when he and his mom could barely afford to keep a rusted Chevy running. Vulnerable women were his weak spot, and he knew that. When it came to Celia and their history, his tendency to protect was all the more powerful.

He monitored the controls, his feet working in tandem with his hands—like playing the piano, it required two-handed coordination along with his feet. He played the chopper through the air, over tiny houses far below. Far above the threat to Celia, for now.

Because no matter how much he wanted her in his bed again—and he wanted that so much it gnawed at his gut—he could not lose sight of his primary goal here. He had to keep her safe. And that meant keeping his libido in check. A more restrained approach once he had her tucked far away from here seemed the better plan than pressing her on that kiss now.

Given her death grip on the seat, it appeared Celia had left her daredevil days behind. Her paling face sucker punched him, making him feel guilty as hell for being cranky with her when she talked about sappy emotions. Love hadn't pulled him out of his messed-up life. He'd put his world on track with practical determination and hard work.

Still, he couldn't stand to see her hurt…

He thumbed the private mic button. "It's going to be

all right, Celia. I swear. We're going to meet up with a school friend of mine at his vacation home in the Florida panhandle. He'll be able to help us slip out of the country without the fanfare, attention and danger of going through an airport."

At least he had her away from Azalea now. One step in the right direction.

She looked away from the windscreen and over at him. "A school friend?"

"Yeah, a few of us have kept in touch." A few? A select few. The ones who worked for Salvatore, a group of pals from school who'd dubbed themselves The Alpha Brotherhood.

"Close friends?"

"Definitely," he said simply. "There were two types of people at that boarding school. Those who wanted a life in the military. And those of us who needed the regimen of a military education."

"You were already incredibly regimented and motivated." Her soft voice caressed his ear, the hum of the helicopter engine fading until he only heard her. "You didn't need that."

"Apparently I did." He couldn't deny it. "Hanging out at bars underage, knocking up my girlfriend. I wouldn't call that succeeding at life."

"I played a part in that." Her voice held so much regret it reached across to him.

"I'm damn lucky I ended up there, where they could straighten me out."

"How bad was the school they sent you to?" Her hands slid from the seat to twist in her lap. "I worried about you."

"Not as bad as jail would have been. I know I was lucky. Like I said, I got a top-notch education, music lessons and discipline." It wasn't what he would have chosen for himself, but he'd made the most of the opportunity, determined to prove himself to all the doubters. "And the major bonus? My mother didn't have to work double shifts anymore."

"Ahhh." Her melodic voice hummed softly. "So you really stayed at the school for your mother."

"You always did see right through me." He checked the controls again, refusing to let the tension knotting his gut affect his skills. "I was so angry back then that I wanted to tell the judge where he could stick his 'deal.' I was innocent and no one was going to label me a drug user. But one look at my mother's face, and I knew I had to accept."

"So you left town."

"I did." He'd left her. That had been the toughest part, knowing she was carrying his child and he'd failed to provide a future for them. "Chances of me walking away from that trial with a clean slate were slim."

She'd already told him she planned to give up the baby, and as wounded as he was by her decision, he had nothing to offer to change her mind. He'd left town. There'd been no reason to stay.

"Tell me about these close friends who are going to help us out?"

A safe enough subject. Most of the press knew who his friends were; they just didn't know the details of what bonded them to each other. "Troy Donavan will be meeting us when we land."

"The Robin Hood Hacker… I didn't expect that."

Troy had hacked into the Department of Defense's computer system as a teen to expose corruption. He'd done the crime and proudly served his time at the military school. If anything, Troy had griped about *not* being sent to jail.

He continued naming. "Conrad Hughes will meet us along the way."

"A casino magnate with questionable ties? And Elliot Starc, as well, playboy race-car driver?" She laughed, but she also sank deeper in her seat. "I'm not feeling all that safe here."

If only she knew...

He explained what he could. "Yes, we landed at that school for a reason and came out better men. If it makes you feel any better, our Alpha Brotherhood includes Dr. Rowan Boothe."

"The philanthropist doctor featured in *People* magazine's 100 Sexiest Men issue? He invented some kind of revolutionary computerized surgical technique..."

"With our computer-expert buddy Troy. Do you trust my friends now?" He glanced over at her and found a twinkle in her eyes.

Damn. She'd played him, getting him to share more than he'd intended. He'd always been susceptible to this woman. She might appear less impulsive, more steady.

But she was every bit as seductive.

Why did everything she learned about Malcolm have to be so blasted appealing?

Celia had worked during the whole helicopter ride to find a flaw in him, and the more he shared about how he'd spent his life since he left Azalea, the more she found to admire about him.

She pulled her eyes off his handsome profile as the helicopter began landing at his friend Troy Donavan's beach house on the Florida Gulf Coast. Apparently the

Robin Hood Hacker allowed choppers to land on his lawn, as well.

What an unexpected friendship. Malcolm had been so straitlaced as a teenager. Although the tabloids certainly painted him as a partying Romeo now.

But she couldn't stop thinking about his saying he'd chosen the reform-school option for his mom rather than fighting the charge. Without question, Celia knew he'd never touched drugs. And she also knew him to be very prideful of how hard he'd worked. To swallow his pride and accept a plea bargain had to have been horribly difficult for him.

This decision to go with Malcolm to Europe grew more complicated by the second—and more enticing. What other secrets might she discover about him? What other nuances were there to the adult man he'd become?

A man who flew a helicopter as adeptly as he played the piano.

The chopper touched down lightly on the lawn with a simple kiss to the earth. The blades rotated overhead, sea grass bending with the rotor gusts. A uniformed guard opened her door and offered a hand to help her out. She snagged her floral tote bag and stepped free, the ground buzzing beneath her feet.

Before she could blink, Malcolm was at her side. His arm looped around her waist, warm and muscular, guiding her not toward the stucco beach mansion but toward a small private airstrip with a Learjet parked and waiting.

She felt as if Alice had just slipped a little farther down the rabbit hole. Her father traveled first-class, and even periodically rented a Cessna, but nothing on as grand a scale as this.

Seconds later, Malcolm palmed her waist as she

stepped inside the luxury aircraft, where another couple waited in the cabin of white leather and polished brass.

A red-haired woman with freckles stood, her hand extended. "You must be Celia. I'm Hillary, Troy's wife."

The wife of the Robin Hood Hacker.

Hillary appeared down-to-earth, blessedly normal, wearing jeans and a T-shirt—no doubt designer given how perfectly they fit. But still, no fake boobs or platinum-bleached hair. Just genuine red hair and freckles with a natural smile.

Already, Malcolm had moved past her to shake hands with a man she recognized from newspaper articles—Troy Donavan, quirky computer mogul who'd once used those skills to breach the cyber walls of the Department of Defense.

She overheard Malcolm's familiar Southern drawl. "Sorry we're late. The drive out took us longer than we expected."

"No worries, brother." Troy led him to a row of computer screens at a corner-office console in the tricked-out jet. "I'll give you a quick update while my wife keeps our lovely guest occupied."

Her eyes lingered on the broad expanse of Malcolm's shoulders, the strong column of his neck exposed as he leaned over the computer.

Hillary touched her lightly on the arm to regain her attention and gestured to a seat. "You look shell-shocked. I'm guessing he didn't take much time to explain. But covering his trail from the press, the fans and whoever has been bothering you had to happen fast."

Celia sank onto the leather sofa and patted along the seat for the belt. They were leaving now? No packing, no passports? No telling her friends… What the hell had she agreed to?

Her gaze tracked back to Malcolm. Who was this man she'd just agreed to leave the country with?

Hillary sat beside her. "We've heard a lot about you from Malcolm."

She looked up quickly, warily. "What did he say?"

"That you're old friends and you're having trouble with a stalker. So he's helping you out."

"He is. I'm lucky," she conceded to Hillary and herself just as the Learjet engines buzzed to life.

The captain's voice piped over the intercom, welcoming them all. All four of them. Not just Malcolm's friend, but Donavan's wife, as well. She hadn't expected Hillary to come along. Did the woman's presence here—the whole "group" outing—mean the romantic signals she'd been getting from Malcolm were wrong?

No wonder he hadn't acted on the kiss.

She should be grateful. The pressure was off since he wouldn't be tempting her. She could tamp down the crazy desire to jump his bones and just chalk it up to nostalgia. She kept right on repeating that to herself as they climbed into the sky, heading for the first stop on Malcolm's European tour.

Except, no matter how many times she told herself otherwise, she couldn't deny the truth. She wanted more, more of Malcolm's kisses. More of *him*.

And there wasn't a chance in hell she could afford to act on that desire.

Seven

The trip across the Atlantic to France passed in a blur for Celia as the time change plunged them into the night. But then her flights usually consisted of delayed connections, long layovers and lost baggage, followed by finding a cab in the heat, rain or snow.

Thanks to Malcolm's influence, she'd experienced superstar posh luxury and speed. Even sending in her grades had seemed surreal as she'd sat at a decked-out business center on the plane, with a cabin steward bringing her tea and fruit.

Now the Learjet was parking at the terminal at the Paris–Charles de Gaulle Airport, the first stop on Malcolm's European tour—with his friends along.

Surprisingly, though, she'd enjoyed getting to know Hillary during the flight, and bottom line, she should be grateful for the distraction. Distraction? Okay, the *chaperone* who would help Celia hold strong in her resolve *not* to plaster herself against Malcolm again in some impulsive moment.

And there were at least a few hundred other chaperones outside waiting under the halo of halogen lights. She glided her fingers down the glass of the window, showcasing legions of fans waving signs that were both handmade and professional.

I heart Malcolm.

Marry me.

Je t'aime.

Police and airport guards formed a human wall between the fans and the carpet being rolled out to the Learjet. Screaming, crying females threw flowers and…

Panties? Ew. Gross.

The gentle hum of the plane stopped, and everyone unbuckled as the steward opened the door. Noise swelled inward, high-pitched cheers, squeals and screams. The words jumbled together, but their adoring enthusiasm for Malcolm Douglas was unmistakable. He was this generation's Harry Connick Jr. and Michael Bublé—times ten.

Chuckling, Troy scooped up a fedora and dropped it on his head. "Dude, I think there's a woman out there who wants you to autograph her breasts."

Malcolm scowled, shrugging on a blue jacket with his jeans and button-down. "We'll just have to tell her I forgot my marker."

Hillary held up her leather portfolio and said with a wicked glint in her eyes, "I'm sure I have one in here you could borrow."

"Not funny." Malcolm smiled tightly.

Celia agreed. The thought of women climbing all over him made her ill.

Troy clapped him on the back. "Where's your sense

of humor, man? You're always quick with the sarcasm when somebody else is stressed."

A joker? He hadn't been that way back in high school. He'd been intense and driven, but never sarcastic or jaded. The fact that his achieving his life's dream hadn't left him unscathed niggled at her.

"I'll be a lot less stressed after we reach the hotel. So let's get moving." Malcolm picked up Celia's floral bag and started to pass it to her.

Troy choked on a cough.

Malcolm looked at him sharply. "What now, Donavan?"

"I just never thought I'd see the day when you carried a woman's purse for her."

Celia snatched it from his hands. "It's not a purse. It's a tote bag for my computer and my wallet. My favorite bag, for that matter. I bought it from the Vera Bradley Collection—" She stopped short, wincing. "I'm not helping you, am I, Malcolm?"

"No worries," he reassured her, planting his hand between her shoulder blades with unsettling ease. "I'm confident enough in my manhood I could carry that pink flowery bag like a man purse straight into that crowd."

"Photo, please?" Troy asked. "I'd pay good money."

Celia watched them joke and laugh together as they made their way to the door, and she realized she'd never seen Malcolm with friends before. Not even eighteen years ago. He'd never had time for recreation then. Between school, work and music lessons, he'd been driven to succeed, to make his mother's hard work pay off even at the expense of any social life most teens expected as their due. What other changes were there in his life now?

They stopped in the open hatch, and the crowd roared to a fever pitch of squeals and screams. He'd earned this, fame and adulation, yet he was still a man at ease with carrying her bag. He waved to the crowd, stirring the cheers even louder.

His hand slid along her spine until his arm went around her waist, cutting her thoughts short with the shock of his solid hold.

"Malcolm?" Halting in the open hatchway, she glanced at him, confused. "What are you doing?"

"This," he warned her a second before sealing his mouth to hers.

So much for worrying about holding strong against kissing him again. He planted a lip-lock on her to end all lip-locks. The familiarity of his mouth on hers tempted Celia, and before she could think, her hand gravitated to his chest. Her fingers curled into the crisp linen of his jacket.

The crowd roared. Or was that her pulse?

Malcolm dipped her ever so slightly back, stroking her face and along her hair before guiding her upright again. Thank goodness he kept his arm around her waist, because her knees were less than steady as he ended the kiss. Her blood pounded in her ears, her fist still clenched along the lapel of his jacket.

"What the hell was that all about?" she hissed softly, trying not to look at his friends grinning behind him.

Malcolm covered her hand with his, his blue eyes holding hers with an intensity she couldn't mistake. "Making sure the world knows you're mine and anyone who touches you will have hell to pay."

He peeled her hand free then locked arms with her, starting down the metal steps onto the concrete. She held on tightly, her legs still wobbly from his kiss in front of a crowd of people and camera lenses. What about him warning her about the possibility of the press seeing them at a B and B? Had he just said that before because he wanted her to go with him?

Her skin chilled in spite of the warm summer breeze, carrying the scent of flowers tossed by fans. A sleek white limousine waited a few strides away.

Desperate to regain her balance, she angled toward Malcolm to whisper, "I thought we were giving off the impression of friends traveling. Casual companions. What about how you worried the press would see us at a hotel?"

"I didn't want to claim you until you were safe."

Safe? Her feelings for him were anything but safe. "Weren't you the one who made fun of puppy love in the limo?"

His cerulean-blue eyes slid over her, soothing like cool water on overheated flesh. "Darlin', this has nothing to do with puppy love and everything to with adult passion. With cameras in our face 24/7, it'll be impossible to carry off a lie. Those photographers will pick up on the fact that I want you so badly my damn teeth hurt."

Her breath hitched in her throat. "I don't know what to say."

He stopped at the limo, waving to the crowds once before he looked at her adoringly again. Totally an act. Right? He waved her into the stretch limousine before following her inside.

"Celia," he said quickly while Troy and Hillary were still outside, "rather than lie about our attraction and make the press all the more desperate to prove what they already sense, it's better just to be honest about this. So be forewarned. I'll be kissing you and touching you and romancing you very publically and very often."

A shiver of anticipation skittered up her spine. How would she ever withstand that kind of romantic assault?

"But I already told you. We can't do this. We can't go back. I'm not climbing into bed with you again."

She willed herself to believe it.

"It won't matter." He kissed the tip of her nose, then whispered against her skin, "Your eyes are crystal clear. The camera will pick up the truth."

She couldn't catch her breath, and her skin flushed where he touched her. Kissed her.

"Do tell, Malcolm. What truth might that be?"

"Darlin', you want me every bit as much as I want you." He stretched an arm along the back of the seat, going silent as Troy and Hillary settled in across from them.

Hillary grinned from ear to ear. "Welcome to Paris, the city of love."

Malcolm stood alone on the hotel balcony overlooking the Eiffel Tower. Celia and the Donavans had already settled into their rooms for the night, turning in now to combat jet lag.

He, however, was too restless to sleep, too caught up in the need to take Celia into his room, his bed. He used to fantasize about bringing Celia to France, taking her to concerts and proposing to her in a place with a view just like this one. Yet another dream that hadn't panned out the way he'd planned.

The whole flight, he'd found his eyes drawn to her again and again. Taking in the waves of her hair draping along her shoulder, even how she chewed her thumbnail while poring over grades, trying to decide whether or not to give a student an extra point for a better letter grade.

Everything about Celia entranced him. It always had. Even when they were kids on a playground, he'd known she was special, a dynamo with an electric personality that people wanted to be around. Other kids gravitated to her open smile, melodic laugh and her willingness to try anything. Even come to stick up for the new kid in the middle of an embarrassing-as-hell asthma attack.

Yet even then, as she'd helped him fish his inhaler out of his backpack, he'd been aware of their differences. For class parties, her mom brought a clown to set up an ice-cream bar, and his mom made cupcakes in their tiny kitchen. Such a strange thing to remember now, especially when money was no longer an issue.

He felt the weight of eyes on him and turned sharply, then relaxed.

Colonel John Salvatore stood in the open doorway, wearing his standard gray suit and red tie. The colonel worked at Interpol headquarters in Lyon, France, so it shouldn't be surprising he'd shown up here. Only surprising he'd arrived in the middle of the night.

"Good evening, sir." Malcolm didn't bother asking how Salvatore had gotten into his suite. "You could have called, you know. Anything new to report?"

"Nothing new." The retired headmaster stepped up beside him at the rail. "Just in town for your concert. Thought I would say hello, Mozart."

Mozart… Back in the day, his classmates had called him by the name of just about every composer out there since he spent so many hours playing classical music. Mostly, he played the classical stuff because it tended to chase off the other students, allowing him some peace in the crowded school.

"I appreciate the extra security, Salvatore. I mean that. I'll rest a lot easier knowing Celia's safe until the authorities can sort out the mess back home."

The colonel loosened his tie and tucked it into his pocket. "Are you sure you know what you're doing?"

With the simple discarding of his tie, Salvatore went from distant boss to caring mentor.

Malcolm shook his head, his eyes locked on the Eiffel Tower glowing in the night. "Hell, no, but I can't back away."

"Do you have some kind of vendetta against her?"

"What?" Malcolm looked back sharply, surprised the man even had to ask. "I would hope you know me better than that."

"I know how troubled you were when you showed up at the school."

"We all were." Angry. Defiant. Wanting to have a normal high-school experience but knowing damn well it was too late to go back.

"You tried to run away three times."

"I didn't want to be locked up," he said, dodging the real reason for why he'd risked everything, even jeopardizing the peace he'd brought his mother.

"You risked jail time leaving." Salvatore leaned his elbows on the railing, the ground seven floors below. Sparse traffic drove by, late-night partiers stepping into the hotel next door.

"But you never reported me." Malcolm still didn't know why, any more than he could figure out why they were discussing this now.

"Because I knew you were one of the few kids sent to that school who were actually innocent."

Malcolm straightened in surprise. He'd never once proclaimed his innocence, and everyone had assumed he was guilty. Everyone except Celia, but even she had pulled away from him in the end. Not that he could blame her. Still, hearing the colonel's unconditional confidence... It meant a lot, then and now. "How can you be so sure?"

"I'd seen enough users and dealers come through that

school to recognize one when he crossed my path. You weren't involved in drugs in any way, shape or form," he said with unmistakable certainty in his voice. "Besides, if you had a drug problem, this lifestyle would have wrecked you long ago." As if to lend weight to his words, drunken laughter drifted up from the street.

"So you believe in me because of your proof."

"The facts merely reinforced my gut. I also know that a man will do anything for his child. I understand. I would die for my kid," he said, offering a rare glimpse into himself. "I figured you took that job at the bar hoping to make enough money to support Celia and your child. You didn't want her to give up the baby, and I'm guessing you wanted to keep the child because your father abandoned you."

"Damn, Colonel." Malcolm stepped back, looking for an escape from the truth. "I thought your doctorate was in history, not psychology."

He'd relived enough of the past since seeing Celia again. He wasn't prepared for this kind of walk down memory lane, especially when the trip was a rough ride that always left him raw.

"Doesn't take a shrink to know you're protective of your mother, and you have reason to resent your biological father. So? Do you have a vendetta to fulfill? Some revenge plan in having Celia close to you?"

"No—hell, no." Malcolm denied it and meant it. The last thing he wanted was to see Celia hurt. "Celia and I are both adults now. And as for our kid, she's almost an adult, as well. So there's no going back. The notion of a redo or revenge is moot."

"Nothing's ever moot. Remember that."

He'd had enough of these pointless jabs at old wounds.

"Why don't we talk about your kid, then? Don't you have a ball game to go to or something?"

"Fine." Salvatore held up his hands. "I'll just spell it out for you. It's all well and good that you want to protect Celia. But you need to accept your feelings for that woman aren't moot if you're ever going to move forward with your life."

And with that parting shot, Salvatore disappeared as silently as he'd appeared, leaving Malcolm alone on the balcony. God, he needed to go inside and sleep, charge up for the performance, protect his voice from the night air.

Instead, he kept right on staring at the Eiffel Tower, battling a bellyful of regrets. Given what Salvatore had said, it didn't sound as if he had much chance of ever putting the past to rest. Try as he might to move on, he still carried a whole lot of guilt about what had happened. More than that, he still had feelings for Celia. Feelings that weren't going to go away just because he tried to ignore them.

In which case, maybe ignoring them was a piss-poor idea. He wasn't getting anywhere like this. So why the hell was he denying himself what he wanted most right now? There was nothing stopping him from persuading Celia to let him back into her bed.

And the concert tomorrow would be the perfect place to begin.

Toying with the twisted seed-pearl necklace, Celia stood backstage at the concert with Hillary as Malcolm gripped the mic, walking along the edge of the stage and serenading the swarms of females reaching up. Their screams combatted with the sound system pumping out his voice and the band. She'd spent a large portion of her life performing, so the lights, the parade of backup instruments and techies didn't faze her. Still, she couldn't help but be awed by the intensity of it all, the energy radiating off the thousands of people who'd come to hear Malcolm Douglas.

He'd been emphatic about her staying backstage. He didn't trust her safety out in the audience, even sitting in one of the exclusive boxes. So she watched from the sidelines, enjoying the sight of him in profile. He wore a black suit and shirt without a tie, his songs a mix of current soft-rock tunes and retro remixes of old classics.

And oh, God, his voice was stirring her every bit as much as his kiss at the airport.

At least she had Hillary to keep her company, along with another friend of theirs, Jayne Hughes. Jayne was apparently married to another reform-school buddy of Malcolm's. They'd all come out in force with their husbands to see him perform—and keep watch over her. Malcolm's friends and their wives were rock-solid loyal, no question.

While Hillary was fresh-faced, freckled and approachable in her jeans and sequined tank top, Jayne was so darn elegant and poised in her simple sheath dress that Celia resisted the urge to check her makeup. She smoothed her damp hands down the loose, silky dress she'd chosen from the racks of clothes Malcolm had ordered sent to her room. He'd been gone all day for sound checks.

The chic, blonde Jayne leaned toward her. "It's a little overwhelming."

Hillary arched up onto her toes for a better view. "And incredible."

Jayne continued, "And overwhelming."

Celia reevaluated her image of Jayne Hughes as a cool socialite as she realized the woman genuinely was worried for her. "You can go ahead and ask."

"Ask what?" Jayne answered.

"Why I'm here. Why I'm with Malcolm." She glanced at him onstage as he took his place behind a grand piano. So many times she'd sat beside him to play in tandem, or accompanied him on the guitar. Their shared appreciation of music had added layers to their relationship back then. "Or maybe you already know the story."

"Only that you and Malcolm grew up in the same town, and you've come here to get away from a stalker at home." Jayne smoothed her already perfectly immaculate hair, shoulder-length and bluntly cut. She looked every bit the casino magnate's wife, adored and pampered. Loved.

Celia shifted her attention back to the stage. Malcolm's smooth baritone washed over her, so familiar even with the richness of maturity adding more flavor to the tone. "We've known each other since we were kids, dated in high school."

Jayne tipped her head to the side. "You're different from the other women he's seen."

She wondered if they referred to the women he'd really dated or the ladies he'd been photographed with for—as he insisted—strictly publicity purposes. Still, she couldn't resist asking, "Different how?"

"You're smart," Jayne answered without hesitation.

Hillary chimed in, "Serious."

"Not clingy," Jayne continued.

Hillary added, "Literate."

They made her sound utterly boring. "Thank you for the…uh…"

"Compliment," Hillary said. "Totally. Malcolm's a lot deeper than he likes to let on."

He was. Or at least, he had been back then. And now? It was tough not to appear too hungry for these nuggets of information about Malcolm's life since they'd been apart.

Jayne tapped her foot lightly to the music, one of Malcolm's more upbeat songs. "I met Malcolm just over seven years ago. In all the time I've known him, he's never made friends beyond his school buddies. Even his manager went to the military academy with him."

Hillary held up a finger. "And he's close to his mother, of course."

Yeah, she knew that and respected him for it even though Terri Lynn had disapproved of her. Okay, more than disapproved. His mother had hated her. Celia smiled tightly, staying quiet.

Jayne's blue eyes slit with sympathy. "You must have been important to him."

"We share a lot of history." Understatement of the year.

"And we're nosy. Just ignore us both, and let's enjoy the concert."

Grateful to have the spotlight off her for now at least, she turned her attention to the stage, where the focus narrowed to a true spotlight on a lone bar stool with a guitar propped against it.

Malcolm sat, his foot on the lowest rung, and settled the guitar on his knee. "I have a new song to share with you tonight, a simple song straight from the heart…."

The heart? She resisted the urge to roll her eyes as she thought of how he'd vowed he didn't believe the love songs he sang. She watched with a new, more jaded perspective.

With the first stroke of his fingers along the strings, Celia gasped. Her stomach knotted in recognition.

Each strum of the acoustic, unplugged moment confirmed her fears, touched her soul and rattled her to her core. A completely low blow, unfair—and designed to bring her to her knees. She didn't know whether to cry or scream as he sang the first notes of the song he'd written for her years ago.

He sang "Playing for Keeps."

Eight

The strains of "Playing for Keeps" echoed in his head even after he'd finished the last encore, reminding him of a time when he'd actually believed that idea. The audience ate up the simple melody and sappy premise.

Exiting stage right, he began to doubt the wisdom of rolling out that old tune to soften up Celia. He couldn't read her face in the shadowy wings, but he damn well knew his insides were a raw mess. Thank God his Alpha Brotherhood buddies were backstage with her, a wall of protection behind her while a couple of the wives kept her company. So his pals had her back—and his—until he could get himself on level ground.

This whole trip down memory lane was a double-edged sword, but he wouldn't lose sight of the goal. He and Celia needed to see this through. To settle the past before they could move forward with the future. The applause and cheers swelling behind him meant nothing if he couldn't find some resolution with Celia.

God, she was gorgeous in a silky sapphire dress with a hint of ruffle teasing her knees. And the plunging neckline—he couldn't look away, especially as throughout the concert she'd toyed with those tiny strands of pearls twisted together. Her feminine curves had always driven him to his knees and drained him of the ability to think. But holy hell, he could feel.

Turned on and turned inside out.

He wanted to have her naked in his arms again more than he wanted air. More than he wanted another concert or even another assignment. Getting into her bed again had become his mission of the moment. She was, and always had been, the woman he wanted more than any other.

As he drew closer to her, though, he realized he'd made a big, big mistake with the song. Her lips were tight, her eyes sparking with anger and something even worse.

Pain.

Crap. The sight of her distress sucker punched him. He'd meant to tap into her emotions, not hurt her.

Stepping into the backstage shadows, he reached out to her. "Celia—"

She held up both hands, keeping an arm's distance between them. "Great concert. Fans adored that new *love* song of yours. Congratulations. Now, if you'll excuse me, I'm ready to turn in for the night. Looks like I have plenty of guards, so you're officially absolved of protective detail."

With a brittle smile, she pivoted on her heel and walked away, pushing through the crowd double-time.

Hillary Donavan studied him with perceptive eyes before nudging Jayne to join her in racing to catch up with

Celia. Bodyguards melted from the backstage melee, encircling the women in an almost-imperceptible bubble of protection.

Malcolm slumped against a pallet of backup amps. How could he win over stadiums full of people yet still be clueless when it came to this one woman?

A hand clapped him on the shoulder, and he damn near jumped out of his skin. Troy Donavan stood beside him to his left, Conrad Hughes to his right. The international casino magnate was a lot less brooding these days since he'd reconciled with his wife.

Troy thumped Malcolm between the shoulder blades again. "Woman troubles?"

"Always," Malcolm said simply.

Troy charged alongside. "My advice? Give her space—"

Conrad interrupted, "But not so long that she thinks you're avoiding her."

Troy continued, "Enough time to cool down about whatever lame-ass thing you did."

Fair enough and true enough, except, "I can't afford to give her space, not with—"

"A stalker." Troy finished his sentence. "Right. She has guards. We'll be in the room next to hers playing cards. Meanwhile, smile your way through the reporters and let's get back to the penthouse."

An offer his stressed-out brain could not resist.

The limo ride through the night streets of Paris with the Arc de Triomphe glowing in the distance was as awkward as hell. With Celia looking anywhere but at him, the others in the vehicle made small talk to fill the empty air.

Finally—thank God, finally—they reached their historic hotel. The women smiled their way past reporters as they charged up the steps between stone lions. And before Malcolm could say "What the hell?" he found himself staring at Celia's closed door in the penthouse suite.

He turned back to the spacious living room connecting all the bedrooms. While he tried not to take the wealth for granted, the carved antiques and gilded wood were wasted on him tonight. His longtime buddies were all doing a piss-poor job of covering their grins.

"Gentlemen." Malcolm scrubbed a hand over his bristled jaw. "There's no reason for the rest of you to hang out here in the doghouse with me. Granted, it's a luxurious doghouse. So enjoy your cards and order up whatever you want on my tab. But I'm done for the night."

Troy straddled a chair at the table in the suite's dining area. "Like hell. We're not letting you check out on us any more than you would let us leave. The rest of our party should be arriving right about—"

The private elevator to the penthouse dinged with the arrival of…

The rest of the party? Crap.

The brass doors slid open in the hall to reveal three men, each one an alumni of the North Carolina Prep School. Alpha Brotherhood comrades. And recruits of Salvatore for Interpol.

Malcolm's concerts gave them the perfect excuse for reunions. First out of the elevator, Elliot Starc, a Formula One driver who'd just been dumped by his fiancée for playing as hard and fast as he drove. Behind him, Dr. Rowan Boothe, the golden-boy saint of the bunch who devoted his life to saving AIDS/HIV orphans in Africa. And lastly, Malcolm's manager, Adam Logan, aka The Shark, who would do anything to keep his clients booked and in the news.

Shoving away from the window, Malcolm shrugged

off his jacket, which still bore the hint of sweat from the concert. "We're gonna need a bigger table."

His manager grinned. "Food and drinks are on the way up." He took his chair at the far side. "There are going to be a lot of brokenhearted fans out there once they realize this thing with Celia isn't just a new fling."

There was no escaping his pals, who knew him so well. Better to meet their questions head-on—and bluff. "Logan, I don't have a clue what you're talking about."

Conrad shuffled the cards smoothly. "Seriously, brother, you're going to play it that way?"

The saintly doctor dropped into a seat. "I thought you were over her."

"Clearly, I'm not," he said tightly and too damn truthfully. Everywhere he looked in the room, he already saw reminders of her—and it was just a hotel room, for God's sake.

Elliot poured himself a drink at the fully stocked bar. "Then why the hell did you stay away for eighteen years? It's all I can do to stay away from Gianna since she gave me my walking papers."

When had his brothers started ganging up on him? "That's the way Celia wanted things then. Now our lives are very different. We've moved on."

His manager tapped his temple. "Two musicians who're obviously attracted to each other. Hmm…still not tracking your logic on being wrong for each other."

"Breaking up was best for her," Malcolm answered, irritation chewing his already churning gut. "I wrecked her life once. I owe it to her not to do that again."

Logan kept right on pressing. "So even though you let her go, you've been making billions to show up her old man."

"Or maybe I enjoy nice toys."

Troy tipped back in his chair, smoothing a hand down his designer tie. "You're sure as hell not spending it on clothes."

"Who appointed you the fashion police?" Malcolm unbuttoned his cuffs and rolled up his sleeves. "Start dealing. I'll be back."

He strode over to the bulletproof window for a better signal and pulled out his phone to check for messages from Salvatore. He'd seen his old mentor in a private box at the performance, a glamorous woman at his side. But even when he socialized, the colonel was never off the clock. Malcolm's email filled with data from Salvatore's intelligence on the principal Celia had been "sort of seeing." His references, his awards and a dozen other ways he was an all-around great guy.

So why didn't he have even partial custody of his kids? Strange, especially for a principal. Malcolm typed an answer to Salvatore then shut down his phone.

He turned, finding the saintly doc lounging in the doorway.

"Damn, Rowan," Malcolm barked, "you could have spoken or something to let me know you were there."

"You sound a little hoarse there, buddy. Is the concert tour already wearing on your vocal cords? I can check you over if you're having trouble."

"I'm fine, thanks." He clipped his phone to his belt, and still Elliot didn't move. "Anything else?"

"As a matter of fact, yes, there is," the golden boy pressed, but then he never gave up trying to fix the world. "Why are you tearing yourself up this way by being with her again?"

"You're the good guy. I would think you'd understand. I let her down once." Malcolm started toward his bedroom door to ditch his sweaty coat and give himself a chance to regain his footing. "I need to make up for that. I have to see this through."

"And you'll just walk away when you figure out who's after her?" he asked, his sarcasm making it all too clear he didn't believe it for a second.

"She doesn't want the kind of life I lead, and no way do I fit into hers now." The last thing he wanted was to go back to Azalea, Mississippi. "I promised myself I wouldn't get involved. What she and I had was just puppy love."

"What happens if someone breaks into her house next month? Or a student lets the air out of her tires? Are you going to come running to her side?"

Rowan's logic set Malcolm's teeth on edge.

"Quit being an ass." He charged past, back into the living room.

His manager leaned back in his chair and called over to him, "Quit being delusional. Either claim the woman or don't. But time to commit to a course."

"Damn it, Adam," Malcolm growled, closing in on the round table. "Do you think you could speak a little softer? I don't think they heard you over in Russia."

He looked down the hallway toward Celia's room. Once he was confident the door wouldn't open with an angry Celia, he sat as Conrad dealt the cards.

"Claim her?" the casino magnate repeated. "I can almost hear my wife laughing at you if she heard that. Brother, they claim us. Body and soul."

Elliot grimaced, "You're sounding like one of those sappy songs of Malcolm's… 'Playing for Keeps'? Really, dude? Be straight with us. You wrote that one to get some action."

Malcolm bit back the urge to haul him out of the chair and punch him the way he'd done when Elliot ran off at the mouth in school. Only the image of Celia's pained face made him hold back, humbling him with how much he'd screwed up somehow. "Hope you're going to be happy growing old alone with your race cars and a cat." He gathered his cards. "Now, are we playing poker or what?"

Even as he pretended to shrug off what his friends had said, he couldn't deny their words had taken root. For tonight, he would let her cool down. But come morning, he needed to quit thinking about seducing Celia and actually get down to the business of romancing his way back into her bed. Romancing her, seducing her, was not the same as falling for her. He could make the distinction and so could Celia.

And by learning that, they could both quit glorifying what they'd shared in the past and move on.

Celia tipped her face toward the morning sun, the boat rolling gently under her feet as it chugged along the Seine River. Hillary Donavan told her they'd set up a private ride for their group to see some of the city before they flew out for the next stop on the tour. Such a large group of friends and their wives. While she understood their school connection, she wondered why Malcom's entourage included such luminaries. Usually artists traveled with lesser folk, always remaining the star of their circle. But Malcolm traveled with very high-placed friends from an array of backgrounds. His lack of ego was…appealing.

Gusts channeled down the canal, fluttering her gauzy blouse against her oversensitive skin. She needed this breather before she saw Malcolm again. He hadn't been in the limo with them this morning, and she'd pushed down the kick of disappointment. No doubt he must be sleeping in, exhausted after the performance.

Taking in the image of the Eiffel Tower set against the

backdrop of the historic city, she appreciated the thought-fulness, as well as the chance to escape the hotel suite. She needed this opportunity to air out her mind before they climbed onto the claustrophobic luxury jet again.

The restless night's sleep hadn't done much to settle her tumultuous nerves over how Malcolm had used that piece of their history—onstage, no less—to play with her emotions. He'd always been driven, but she'd never expected him to be ruthless. Her hair lifting in the breeze, she gripped the brass railing of the boat powering along the canal.

"Why are you ignoring me?" a male voice rumbled behind her.

Malcolm's voice.

Rich, intoxicating tones that sent a shiver down her spine.

Her toes curled in her sandals.

Celia turned on her heel to face him, leaning back against the rail. How much longer before his voice stopped making her knees go shaky? Plus the sight of him? Equally dreamy. The past and present blended in his look of faded jeans with designer loafers and a jacket. He wore a ball cap and sunglasses, likely to hide his identity, but she would have known him anywhere.

And just her luck, all of his buddies were making tracks to the other side of the boat, leaving her here. Alone. With Malcolm.

She blinked back the sparks of the morning sun behind his broad shoulders. "I thought you were still at the hotel asleep when I left."

"I came to the boat ahead of the rest of you, slipped on board with the boat captain to reduce the chances of the press finding me." He captured a lock of her hair trailing in the wind and tucked it behind her ear. "Back to my question. Why did you avoid me *last night,* after the concert?"

"Ignoring you?" She angled her head away from his stirring touch. "Why would I do that? We're not in junior high school."

"You haven't spoken to me since those few brief—vague—words after the concert last night." He frowned, shoving his hands into the pockets of his jeans. "Are you pissed because I kissed you on the plane?"

"Should I be upset that you kissed me without asking?" A kiss that still made the roots of her hair tingle. "Or should I be angry about the photos of us together plastered all over tabloids and magazines? Oh, and let's not forget TV gossip shows. We're—and I quote—'The Toast of Paris.'"

"So that is why you've refused to talk to me." He pressed a thumb against his temple, just below the ball cap.

"Actually, I got over that. But the way you mocked me by playing a song you wrote about us in high school—" her anger gained steam "—a song you recently called a puppy-love joke? Now, *that* made me mad."

"Damn it, Celia." He hooked a finger in a belt loop on her jeans and tugged her toward him. "That wasn't my intention."

"Then what did you intend?" she asked, unable to read his eyes behind those sunglasses. She flattened her palms on his chest to keep from landing flush against him, body to body. Still, with their faces a breath apart, her heart skipped a beat.

"Hell, I just wanted to pay tribute to what we shared as teenagers. Not to glorify it, but certainly not to mock it," he said with unmistakable sincerity. "We did share something special back then. I think we can share that again."

Air wooshed from her lungs, making it almost impossible to talk. The sound of the flowing water alongside the boat echoed the roar of blood rushing through her veins. Her fingers curled in the warmth of his jacket. "You missed the mark big-time in getting your meaning across on the stage, Malcolm."

"Let me make it up to you." Pulling off the shades, he rested his forehead against hers, the power of his deep blue gaze bathing her senses.

"You don't have to do anything. You're protecting me from a stalker. If anything, I owe you." She squeezed his jacket tighter. "But that's all I owe you."

His hand slid around her. "I don't want you feeling indebted to me."

Her face tipped to his, so close to kissing, so close to bliss. Her mouth tingled in anticipation. It was getting tougher and tougher to remember why this was a bad idea. The roaring of the water and her pulse grew louder and louder until she realized it wasn't the river or her heartbeat.

"Damn it, the press," Malcolm barked softly, stepping back and sliding his sunglasses on again.

Paparazzi ran along the shore with cameras in hand. Shouts carried on the wind, disjointed phrases.

"—Douglas."

"Kiss her—"

Celia raced alongside him toward the captain's cabin. "I thought you intended for us to kiss for the camera."

"Changed my mind," he called, pulling open the door. "Keeping you happy suddenly became a higher priority."

He tucked her inside, the boat captain glancing over in surprise. Malcolm waved for him to carry on. Apparently Elliot Starc hadn't him given boat-driving lessons, too, she thought, hysterical laughter starting to bubble inside her. Her nerves were seriously fraying.

"What now?" she asked.

Malcolm nodded to the floral bag dangling from her arm. "You could answer your phone."

She looked down fast, the chiming surprising her until she almost jumped out of her skin. "I didn't even hear it."

Fishing inside, she dug through until her hand closed around the phone. She pulled it out and saw her father's number blinking on the screen.

"Hello, Dad. What do you need?"

"Just checking on my baby girl," he said, concern coating every word, "making sure you're all right. I, uh, saw the newspapers this morning."

She grimaced, avoiding Malcolm's eyes. "I'm fine. The pictures were…staged. It's all a part of making sure everyone knows I'm very well protected here in Malcolm's entourage."

"Staged, huh?" her father answered skeptically. "I never knew you were a theater person, because that was some mighty fine acting in the photo."

Her chest tightened with every word from her father. "I don't know what more I can tell you."

"Well, I've been fielding calls all day."

"From the press?" The thought of them hounding her dad made her swallow hard—not easy to do when she was finding it tougher and tougher to breathe.

"My number's unlisted. You know that. The calls are from your friends at school, even that high-school principal you went out with a couple of times."

"I didn't go out with him." She glanced at Malcolm quickly as the enormity of this washed over her. Being with Malcolm now had changed her life in ways she could never undo. Her ordered existence was falling apart. She was losing control—but for once, that didn't seem to be such a bad thing. "We just happened to sit together at events we both attended for work."

"Who drove?"

"Stop it, Dad," she snapped, then backtracked, guilt pinching her. She started pacing restlessly in the small cabin. "I love you, and I appreciate your concern, but I'm an adult."

"Malcolm's standing there with you, isn't he?"

"Why does that matter?" And why couldn't she bring herself to just end the call? God, she hated being caught between them again.

Her father sighed through the phone lines. "Just protect yourself, Celia. You'll always be my baby girl."

His voice stirred more guilt as she thought of his pain over losing his oldest daughter. She pressed a hand to her head, dizzy from lack of breakfast and, yes, pangs of guilt. She thought of her own ache for the baby she'd given up, but at least she knew her child was alive somewhere, growing up loved. Worrying for her father heaped on top of her nerves, which were already stretched to the max by trying to sort through her feelings for Malcolm.

"Dad, I promise I'm being very careful." She measured her words carefully, trying not to let her perceptive father hear the quaver in her voice. "And you? Are you okay? Have you gotten any threatening messages?"

"I'm fine. Blood pressure is in the good zone, and there hasn't been so much as a peep of a threat."

"Thank God," she said, praying that wouldn't change. "I really do appreciate the call. Love you, Dad."

Her heartbeat sped up, new worries crowding her head and making her chest feel tight. Oh, no. She knew the old symptoms. Knew what might happen next if she didn't pull it together.

She thumbed the off button and dropped her phone back into her Vera Bradley bag with shaky hands. "Well, your plan is working. The whole world—even my father—thinks we're having an affair." She gasped for air, trying to fight down the encroaching panic and not succeeding all that well. "Do you think we could just go back to the hotel?"

"Are you okay?" Malcolm asked, just before she could have sworn the boat began listing to the side.

Ah, hell. She reached for Malcolm's hand just before she blacked out.

Nine

Disoriented, Celia pushed through the fog back to consciousness, confusion wrapping around her. Was it morning? Was she at home? No… She was in a *car*.

With each deep breath she inhaled, she drew in the essence of Malcolm. She knew he was beside her.

The past merged with the present, bringing memories of another time she'd fainted. When she was sixteen, she'd snuck out of her room at midnight to meet Malcolm when he finished at the burger joint where he worked after school. She'd been skipping meals because of nausea, and it had been all she could do to stay awake to meet him as promised. But talking to him had been so important. She'd needed to tell him before her parents saw the signs. Before she started to show. But before she could finish telling him, she'd passed out.

Malcolm had rushed her to the emergency room, where of course the doctor called her parents. She squeezed her eyes closed tighter even now over the explosion of anger that had erupted in that E.R. over her pregnancy. Malcolm had insisted they get married. Her father had lunged at Malcolm. Her mother had sobbed.

Celia had wanted to die....

Well, at least she knew for damn sure she wasn't pregnant now. She'd blacked out for an entirely different reason.

Slowly, she took in the feel of the leather seat of the limousine. She must have been carried and put inside. The sounds of the voices around her steadied and the cause of this fainting spell gelled in her mind. She'd been freaking out and gasping for air until she passed out on the boat. Her eyes snapped open. She was inside a limousine with Malcolm and his entire entourage of alumni pals.

He leaned over her, stroking back her hair. His buddy Dr. Rowan Boothe had her wrist in his hand, taking her pulse. The rest of their friends loomed behind them, her world narrowing to this stretch limo with tinted windows and a lot of curious, concerned faces.

How incredibly embarrassing.

She pushed up onto her elbow, sitting. "What time is it? How long have I been—"

"Whoa, whoa, hold on..." Malcolm touched her shoulders and glanced at Rowan. "Doc?"

"Her pulse is normal." Rowan set her hand aside and tucked himself back onto a seat. "I don't see any reason to go to the E.R. I can check her over more thoroughly once we're on the plane to Germany."

Malcolm moved closer again, looking unconvinced. "Are you sure you're okay? What happened back there?"

"I'm fine." She sat up straighter, blinking fast as she tried to regain equilibrium. "Probably just low blood sugar from skipping breakfast."

The lie tasted bad on her tongue. But admitting the truth? Explaining her lingering battle with panic attacks? She wasn't ready to share that.

Malcolm seemed to accept her explanation, though. His shoulders relaxed a little as he opened the mini-fridge. He passed her a bottle of orange juice and a protein bar. "No offense, beautiful, but you don't look okay."

She twisted off the cap and sipped, just to appease him and make her story more believable. What she really needed were some breathing exercises or her emergency meds. Or a way to distance herself from all the feelings Malcolm was stirring up.

She looked out the window as they drove along the shore of the Seine River.

He eyed her for five long heartbeats. "We used to understand each other well, from the second on the playground when you threw sand at that kid for making fun of my asthma attack. Now, though, I want the chance to fight back for you."

Without another word, he gave her the space she'd requested and took a seat at the far end of the stretch limo. Quite a long way. Especially with all of his friends, plus Hillary and Jayne, sitting between them and trying to pretend there wasn't a thick, awkward silence all the way to the airport.

Once the Learjet was airborne to fly them to Berlin, Malcolm continued to honor her request for space, which was actually the best way to get closer to her again. Did he remember that from their past? She fished in her floral bag for her eReader to pass the time and calm her nerves, still jangled from the incident on the boat. She had to steady herself before she ran the gauntlet for the next concert. She pulled the reader case out, her fingers fumbling with the zipper.

Dr. Boothe knelt in front of her, taking the case from her hand and opening it before setting the eReader beside her. "Want to tell me what's wrong?"

She glanced around the plane. Everyone else seemed occupied with the business station or talking in the next cabin. Hillary, an event planner, was in deep conversation with Jayne about a fundraiser in the works for Dr. Boothe's clinic—where apparently Jayne worked, as well. Even the steward was busy readying lunch in the galley.

Turning back to the fair-haired doctor, she said carefully, "I already told Malcolm. I forgot to eat breakfast, but I'm feeling better now," but he still didn't move away. "I'm just going to read until lunch. Thank you."

He picked up her wrist. "Your pulse is still racing and you're struggling for breath."

"You said back at the limo that my pulse rate was fine." She tugged her hand away.

"It wasn't Malcolm's business unless you chose to tell him."

"Thank you." She picked up her eReader pointedly. "I'll let you know if I have a heart attack. I promise."

He shifted to sit beside her. "I don't think that's what's going on here, medically speaking."

Of course it wasn't, but she didn't particularly want to trot out the details of how she'd screwed up and left her medicine at home. She didn't need it all the time, and it had been so long since she'd reached for an antianxiety pill, she'd hoped...

Dr. Boothe stretched out his legs, as if in the middle of some casual conversation. "We can make this a patient/doctor thing, and then I can't say a word to anyone else. The whole confidentiality issue."

She shot a quick look at him, and he seemed...nonjudgmental.

Weighing her options, she decided it was better to trust him and hope he could help her rather than risk another embarrassing incident. "I'm fighting down a panic attack. I left home so quickly I didn't have a chance to get my, uh, medicine. I don't have to take anything regularly anymore, but I do have a prescription for antianxiety medication. The bottle just happens to be sitting in my bathroom cabinet."

A big oversight given that she had a stalker on her tail. But oddly, the thought of being in danger like that wasn't half as scary as the resurrection of her old feelings for Malcolm. The memories of what they'd given up. She hadn't realized how deeply this time with him might affect her.

She hadn't *wanted* to admit it.

Rowan nodded slowly. "That's problematic. But not insurmountable. Your doctor can call in the prescription."

She had already thought of that. "Malcolm is so worried about the stalker back home that I can't make a move without him noticing. It's not that I'm ashamed or anything. I'm just not ready to tell him yet."

"Understood," he said simply, the window behind him revealing a small and distant Paris below. "If you'll give your doctor permission to speak with me, I can take care of a prescription."

"Thank you." The tightness in her chest began to ease at the notion of help on the horizon.

"If you don't mind my asking, when did these attacks begin?"

She recognized his question for what it was, an attempt to help talk her down. "After I broke up with Malcolm. I've had some trouble with depression and anxiety. It's not a constant, but under times of extreme stress…"

She blew out a slow breath, searching for level ground and some control over her racing pulse.

"This sure qualifies as a time of stress, with the threats back home and all the insanity of Malcolm's life."

As the engine hummed through the sky, she thought about the patients he saw on a regular basis in Africa, of their problems, and felt so darn small right now. "You treat people with such huge problems. I probably seem whiny to you, the poor little rich girl who can't handle her emotions."

"Hold on." He raised a hand. "This isn't a competition. And as I'm sure your own doctor has told you, depression and anxiety disorders are medical conditions like diabetes. Serotonin or insulin, all chemicals your body needs. And you're wise to keep watch over your health."

"But your patients—" She stopped short as Malcolm stepped away from the business center. She picked up her eReader. "Thanks, Dr. Boothe, for checking on me. I appreciate your help."

She powered up her book and pretended to read the most recent download from her book club. If only she could act her way through the rest of her problems.

But when it came to Malcolm, she'd never been all that adept at hiding her feelings—feelings that were escalating with him in such close proximity. No question, the man disrupted her well-ordered world, and she feared where that could lead.

Yet, she couldn't bring herself to say goodbye.

His suite in downtown Berlin looked much the same as their digs in Paris, except with less gild to the antiques. But then his tours usually became a blur of hotel rooms and concert halls. God knew his attempt at a bit of sightseeing for Celia in Paris hadn't played out that well. He needed to step back and rethink how to win her over.

Starting with clearing out his well-meaning, advice-peddling pals. They interfered with his plans to get Celia alone. He'd thanked them for gathering around him when he'd called them to help build a wall of protection around Celia as the concert tour started, and he appreciated their ready turnout. But the need for their help had passed. Once they left Germany, his friends would be peeling off, returning to their lives.

At least his concert in Berlin tonight had gone off without a hitch since he'd left "Playing for Keeps" off the playlist. He scanned the living room full of his friends until his eyes landed on Celia curled in a chair, her head resting on her arm as she listened to Troy turn storyteller about their school days, sharing a tale about Elliot Starc since the race-car driver had left earlier.

Not much longer and Malcolm would have Celia all to himself. Finally, they would be alone, aside from his manager. Logan knew how to make himself scarce, though, probably keeping busy working the next angle for his client. Malcolm felt like a jerk for wishing they would all hit the road now.

Part of his impatience could have something to do with what great buddies Celia and Rowan had become. More than once today, they'd sat in a corner, their heads tucked close in conversation. The good doc had even brought her a bag of pastries to make sure she ate enough.

Hell, yes, Malcolm was jealous. The guy had pastries, and Malcolm didn't even have a hint of a plan for what to do next as far as Celia was concerned. His other plans had backfired—kissing for the press, singing "Playing for Keeps." So he did what he did best. He lost himself in music, while staring at Celia's beautiful face. He hitched his guitar more securely on his knee and plucked strings softly while Troy continued his story.

"My senior year—" Troy twirled his fedora on one finger as he talked "—Elliot was new to the school and wanted to impress us, so he hot-wired one of the laundry trucks and smuggled us all out for the night. We snuck into a strip club."

Hillary snagged her husband's spinning hat from his finger. "Strip club? Seriously? This is the story you choose to tell?"

Jayne laughed softly, snuggling into the crook of her husband's arm. "Someone's sleeping alone tonight."

Troy spread his hands wide. "Let me finish. We quickly figured out the club wasn't anything like we'd seen in the movies. The women looked…weary. A couple of the guys wanted to stay but most of us left and went to a pancake house that stayed open all night."

Malcolm remembered the night well. He'd opted to stay in the truck, in a crummy mood because it was Celia's birthday and he resented like hell that he remembered. He'd been aching for her.

Not much had changed.

Hillary dropped her husband's hat onto her head. "I'm not sure I believe you."

Troy kissed his wife's head. "I would never lie to you, babe."

Hillary rolled her eyes. "I'm assuming Elliot went with them to the pancake house since otherwise how would you have gotten the truck started?"

Conrad raised his hand. "Me, too, for the record. I did not stay at the strip club, just so we're clear. I had pancakes with blueberry syrup, extra bacon on the side. Waitresses fully clothed."

Jayne thunked him in the stomach. "Enough already."

Their ease with each other reminded Malcolm of what he and Celia once had—and lost.

Celia hugged a throw pillow. "Why did Elliot end up at the school?" She glanced at Malcolm. "Is that okay to ask?"

"It's in his public bio, so it's no secret." Malcolm sat in the wingback chair beside her—before Rowan could claim the seat—and continued to strum the guitar idly, playing improvised riffs and breathing in the praline-sweet scent of her. "His Wikipedia page states that Elliot was sent to the school for stealing cars. In reality, he took his stepfather's caddy out for a spin and smashed it into a guardrail."

The calm seeped from Celia's face. "Seems like a rather extreme punishment for a joyride."

Malcolm slowed his song, searching for a way to steer the conversation in another direction so she would smile again.

Troy answered, "Multiple joyrides. Multiple wrecks. His stepfather was beating the crap out of him. He wanted to get caught or die. Either way, he was out of his house."

Celia leaned forward. "Why wasn't his stepfather stopped and prosecuted?"

"Connections, a family member on the police force. Lots of warnings, but nothing happened."

Her lips went tight, and she shook her head. "His mother should have protected him."

"Damn straight," Troy agreed. "But I'm sliding off my path here. Let's get back to more entertaining brotherhood tales, like the time a few of us were stuck staying at school over Christmas break. So we broke into Salvatore's office, spread dirt on the floor and tossed quick-grow grass seed. He had a lawn when he returned. He knew we did it, but the look on his face was priceless...."

Malcolm started strumming again, adding his own impromptu score to Troy's tales, but his brain was still stuck on the moment Celia asked why Elliot's mother hadn't protected him. Her reaction was so swift, so instinctive he couldn't avoid the image blaring in his brain. An image of Celia as the mother of his child, fiercely doing everything in her power to protect their baby. He'd been so frustrated—hell, angry—for so long over losing the chance to see his kid that he hadn't fully appreciated how much she'd been hurt.

And damn it all, that touched him deep in his gut in a way that had nothing to do with sex. Right now, he had less of a clue about what to do with this woman than he had eighteen years ago.

The next night, after Malcolm's concert in the Netherlands, Celia put together a late-night snack in their suite. Foraging through the mini-fridge, she found bottles of juice, water and soda, along with four kinds of cheese. She snagged the Gouda and Frisian clove to go with the crackers and grapes on the counter.

Yes, she was full of nervous energy since Malcolm's friends had all gone home. Now she was finally alone with him. How strange that she'd resented their presence at first and now she felt antsy without the buffer they'd provided. Malcolm's manager had stood backstage with her at the concert tonight in Amsterdam. But Logan had his own room here on another floor.

Not that Malcolm had pressured her since they'd checked into the posh hotel. In fact, since her panic attack during the Seine River tour, he'd backed off. On the one hand, she'd wanted him to quit tempting her, but on the other it hurt to think he was turned off by her anxiety.

They had a two-bedroom suite with a connecting sitting room. He was showering, the lights having been particularly powerful—and hot—tonight at yet another sold-out show.

As she heard the shower in the next room stop, she arranged the food on a glazed pottery tray to keep her hands busy and her thoughts occupied with something other than wondering how different the adult, naked Malcolm looked. And what he thought of the "adult" her. She smoothed her hands down her little black dress, lacy, with a scalloped hem that ended just above the knee. Should she rush and change?

She shook off vanity as quickly as she kicked off her heels and loosened her topknot. Lifting the tray with food and a pot of tea, she angled around the bar, past the baby grand piano and into the living area.

Overall the room was brighter, lighter than the other places they'd stayed, the Dutch decor closer to her personal style. On her way past, she dipped her head to sniff the blue floral pitcher full of tulips. She placed the tray on top of the coffee table and curled up on the sofa with her tea. She'd made a pot with lemon and honey to soothe Malcolm's throat after three straight nights of concerts. He had to be feeling the effects.

The door to his bedroom opened, and her eyes were drawn directly to him. So drawn. Held. He stood barefoot, wearing a pair of jeans and T-shirt that clung to his damp skin. His hair was wet and slicked back. And God, did her hands ache to smooth over those damp strands.

What else did she want?

Silly question. She wanted to sleep with Malcolm again, to experience how it would feel to be with him as a woman. All the tantalizing snippets his friends had shared of his past and present drew her in, seducing her with both the Malcolm he'd been and the Malcolm he'd become. She burned to sleep with him, and she couldn't come up with one good reason why she shouldn't.

Would she have the courage to throw caution to the wind and act on what she wanted? "I made us something to eat—as well as tea with lemon and honey to soothe your throat."

"Thanks, but you don't have to wait on me," he answered, his voice more gravelly than usual, punctuating her point about the need for tea. He walked deeper into the room, his hand grazing a miniature wooden windmill, tapping the blades until they spun in a lazy circle.

"Direct orders from your manager," Celia said. "You're to have something to eat and drink, protect your health for the tour."

"What about you? Any more dizzy spells today?" He sliced off a sliver of Gouda. "Here…have some cheese."

She rested her fingers on his wrist, a small move, just a test run to see how he would react. "I'm good. I promise. Your pal the doctor gave me two thumbs up."

Malcolm eyes narrowed before he tossed the cheese into his mouth and paced restlessly around the room, past the baby grand piano, a guitar propped against the side. "You two seemed to hit it off."

Wondering where he was going with the discussion of Rowan, she poured another cup of steaming-hot tea. "What exactly did he invent?"

Malcolm dropped onto the other end of the sofa and reluctantly took the tea. "He devised a new computerized diagnostic model with Troy. They patented it, and they both made a bundle. Essentially, Rowan can afford to retire if he wishes."

Interesting, but not surprising given what she'd gleaned about Malcolm and all his friends. "And he chose to work in a West African clinic instead. That's very altruistic of him."

"You can join the Rowan Boothe fan club. It's large." She lifted an eyebrow in shock. "You don't like him?"

"Of course I do. He's one of my best friends. I would do anything for him. I'm acting like a jealous idiot because you two seemed to hit it off." He tossed back the tea, then cursed over the heat. He set the cup down fast and charged over to the mini-fridge for bottled water.

He was jealous? Of her and Rowan? Hope fluttered.

She set her cup down carefully. "Your charitable donations have been widely reported. Every time I saw you at an orphanage or children's hospital… I admire what you've done with your success, Malcolm, and yes, I have kept up with you the way you've kept up with me."

Malcolm downed the bottle of water before turning back to her. "Rowan's the stable, settle-down sort you keep swearing you want now. But damn it all, I still want you. So if you want him or someone like him, you'd better speak up now, because I'm about five seconds away from kissing you senseless."

"You silly, silly man." She pushed to her feet and walked toward him. "You have nothing to be jealous of. I was asking for his medical help."

"What did you say?" He pinned her with a laser stare. "Are you ill? God, and I've been hauling you from country to country."

"Malcolm, stop. Listen. I have something I need to tell you." She drew in a bracing breath and willed her fluttering pulse to steady. Before they got to the kissing-senseless part, she needed to be sure he was okay with what had happened during the boat ride. Trusting him—anyone—with this subject was tough. But she hoped she could have faith in the genuine, good man she'd seen earlier with his friends. "I was having a regular, old-fashioned panic attack."

He blinked uncomprehendingly for a few seconds before clasping her shoulders. "Damn it, Celia, why didn't you tell me, instead of—"

She rested a hip against the baby grand piano. "Because you would have acted just like this, freaking out, making a huge deal out of it, and believe me, that's the last thing I could have handled yesterday."

Comprehension slid across his leanly handsome face. "Rowan helped you. As a doctor." He plowed his fingers through his hair. "God, I'm such an idiot."

"Not an idiot. Just a man." She sighed with relief to finally have crossed this hurdle without a drawn-out ordeal. "I left my medicine at home. He helped connect with my doctor and get my prescription refilled."

"You've had panic attacks before?"

"Not as often as I used to, but yes, every now and again."

His shoulders rolled forward as he rubbed his forehead. "The concert tour was probably a bad idea. What was I thinking?"

"You had no way of knowing because I didn't tell you." She couldn't let him blame himself. She stroked his forehead for him, nudging aside his hand. Just a brief touch, but one that sent tingles down her arm. "Staying home with some criminal leaving dead roses in my car wasn't particularly pleasant, either. For all we know, I would have had more anxiety back home. You've taken on a major upheaval in your life to help me."

"Are you okay now?" He reached for her, stopping just short of touching her as if afraid she would break.

"Please don't go hypercautious with me." She eased back to sit on the piano bench. "I felt much better after a good night's sleep. The medicine isn't an everyday thing. Not anymore. The prescription is just on an as-needed basis. And while I needed help yesterday, today's been a good day."

He sat beside her, his warm, hard thigh pressing against her. "When did the panic attacks start? Is that okay to ask?"

Gathering her thoughts grew tougher with the brush of his leg against hers. "I had trouble with postpartum depression after... The doctor said it was hormonal, and while the stress didn't help, it wasn't the sole cause—" she pointed at him "—so don't start blaming yourself."

He clasped a hand around her finger, enfolding her hand in his. "Easier said than done."

"You are absolved." She squeezed gently, her heart softening the rest of the way for this man. She'd never had any luck resisting him, and she wondered why she'd ever assumed now would be different. "And I mean that."

"After what happened yesterday, I'm not so sure I can buy into that." Guilt dug deep furrows in his lean face.

"You have to." She cupped his cheek in her palm, the bristle of his late-day beard a seductive abrasion against her palm. Until, finally, she surrendered to the inevitable they'd been racing toward since the minute he'd walked back into her life again. "Because I desperately want to make love with you, and that's not going to happen if you're feeling guilty or sorry for me."

Ten

Malcolm wondered what the hell had just happened.

He'd been turning himself inside out to come up with a plan to romance Celia back into his bed, except then he'd been derailed by thoughts that Rowan was a better man for her, then by concerns for her health and how best to approach her in light of all she'd just told him.

Instead, she propositioned him when he was doing… absolutely nothing.

God, he would never understand Celia Patel. He'd also never been able to turn her down. "Are you sure this is what you want? It's been a stressful couple of days and I want you to be certain."

"I may have had a panic attack yesterday, but I am completely calm and certain of this." Her fingers curved around the back of his neck, her touch cool, steady… seductive. "You and I need to stop fighting the inevitable. I could have sworn you felt the same."

"I do." His answer came out hoarse and ragged, and that had nothing to do with hours of singing. No second thoughts, he reached for her. He gathered her against him. Finally, he had her in his arms again.

Kissing her was as natural as breathing. She sighed her pleasure and agreement, her lips parting for him. A hint of lemon and honey clung to her tongue. His body went harder, his need for her razor-sharp after so damn long without her. No matter how many years had passed, he'd never forgotten her or how perfect she felt in his arms. Better yet, how perfect she felt coming apart in his arms.

Pulling her closer, he stood, guiding her to her feet, as well. Her fingers plowed through his hair, tugging lightly, just hard enough to increase the pleasure. She took his mouth as fully as he took hers. Owning. Stamping possession of each other.

The press of her body against him, the roll of her hips against his, the soft give of her full breasts against his chest ramped up his pulse rate. The heat of her reached through their clothes, tempting him with how much hotter they would feel skin to skin.

His hands roved up her back, into her hair—this woman had the most amazing mass of hair. The curls tangled around his fingers as if every part of her held him, caressed him. He swept the tangled mass over her shoulder and found the top of her zipper. He tugged the tab down the back of her lacy black dress, stroking along her spine as he revealed inch after inch of the softest skin. The scent of her soap, her light fragrance, teased him, and he dragged in a deep breath to take it in.

Hungry to feel more of her, he tucked his hands in the open V of her dress and palmed the satin-covered globes of her bottom. He guided her hips closer as she rocked against him in response, the perfect fit sending his pulse throbbing louder in his ears. The sound of her ragged breathing stoked the heat in him higher, hotter as he kissed along her jaw, the delicate shell of her ear. She whispered her need for more, faster, and damned if he could scrounge the restraint to hold back.

Later, once they'd both taken the edge off, he would go slower. Oh, so much slower, taking his time rediscovering her all night long with his hands and his mouth.

He stroked up her back again, enjoying the goose bumps of pleasure rising on her skin. Cupping her shoulders, he slid the sleeves of her gown to the side, baring her skin and the satin straps of her bra. She was even more damn beautiful than he remembered, with pinup-girl curves that all but sent him to his knees from aching to be inside her again.

A growl of possessiveness rolled up his throat as he peeled the lacy dress down her body, revealing those curves that had threatened to drive him to his knees. He nipped and tasted along her satin bra, kneeling and taking the center clasp between his teeth for a sensual instant before releasing it again, leaving it in place. For now. He skimmed the dress farther down. Fabric hitched on her hips. Pressing his face to her stomach, he inhaled more of her floral scent.

"Cecelia Marie." He sighed her whole name against her, repeating again and again.

Her fingers tangled in his hair, a flush of desire spreading over her skin, encouraging him to continue. He swept her gown down to pool around her bare feet, and ah, she wore black thigh-highs that just begged for him to peel one, then the other, down her smooth legs. He gathered the shimmery hose in his hand, soaking in the residual heat of her before he set them reverently aside.

He rocked back on his heels and took in the sight of

her in black satin panties and a bra. His fantasies didn't look this good, and he'd fantasized about this woman many, many times.

"Malcolm?" A quaver threaded through her voice before she steadied it. "Are you going to sit there all night? Because I have urgent plans for you."

"Plans?" He laughed softly, grateful she didn't intend to roll out questions or doubts. She was keeping things light. "Tell me more."

"Plans for us on the sofa, in the shower and, eventually, in the bed. But the more I talk, the more time we waste. So come back up here and I'll start showing you instead." She tugged him to his feet again to kiss her.

Not that he needed much persuasion to claim her plump mouth. To claim her.

Her tongue met his in bold, familiar touches and strokes. She tugged at his T-shirt, easing back only long enough to yank it over his head. The gust of the air conditioner cooled his overheated flesh, and then she touched him. The feel of her hands against his stomach, along the fastening of his jeans, threatened to send him over the edge. He'd never been good at self-control with her. That thought alone offered enough of a splash of cold water for him to think rationally.

To be smart.

To protect her in the way he hadn't before.

"One second. Wait." He stepped back, his breathing ragged.

"Are you kidding me?" She sagged against the baby grand, and the sight of her in that pose gave him even more ideas about how he planned to spend this night.

Once he took care of one very important detail.

"Birth control," he called as he backed toward his

room, holding up a hand. "Stay right where you are. As you are. Don't move." He smiled. "Please.

A quick sprint to his suitcase, and he returned with a condom in hand. Only to halt in his tracks, mesmerized to his core. Celia had been beautiful and sexy as a teenager. She was a gorgeous, sensual woman now.

She still leaned against the baby grand as he'd requested, her satin underwear a bold contrast to her skin. Her long, dark wavy hair draped over her shoulder, skimming her skin the way he intended to very, very soon.

He tore off his jeans and boxers on the way over to her, but not nearly fast enough. Her mouth curved into a sultry smile as she eye-stroked the erection straining against his stomach. She stretched out an arm and stopped him from pressing flush against her.

Holding his gaze deliberately, seductively, she thumbed open the center clasp of her bra and let the straps slide the rest of the way off until the scrap of satin dropped to the floor. She swept away her panties and kicked them to the side.

"Celia," he groaned, "you're absolutely slaying me."

Her smile wavered. "I assure you, the feeling is entirely mutual. It always has been."

His mouth dried up, and he reached out to skim the back of his knuckles along the curve of her breasts. His body throbbed impossibly harder at just one touch to her naked flesh. And then both her palms flattened against his chest, her nails grazing him lightly—down, then up again to curl around his shoulders. She urged him toward her, body to body, his hard length flat against her stomach, and he almost came undone right then. He needed to regain control, and soon. That fantasy he'd envisioned when he'd seen her posed against the piano came blazing through his mind again, an image he could make a reality now.

He eased his body from her, still holding her face, kissing her until the very last second. And once more. Her hands grappled to hold on to him, and he almost gave in. But he had a mission.

Trailing a hand along her stomach, he walked around to the side of the piano, removed the prop and closed the sleek ebony lid.

Celia tipped her head to the side. "Care to clue me in on what you're doing?"

He clasped her waist and lifted her onto the piano. "I'm doing this. Any objections?"

Her eyes lit with approval. "None whatsoever."

He stepped closer, parting her legs with his body. Her ankles hooked around his back, and she drew him in with the press of her heels. Her arms looped around his neck. She kissed him fully, with a maturity and passion that made their teenage affair fade in his memory. This moment with her, now, the passion combusting between them, burned away everything else.

She was his again.

The impact of that reality thrummed through his veins. He kissed along her jaw, down the vulnerable curve of her neck. He took his time with her breasts even though he ached with the need to be inside her.

But he needed to be certain she was every bit as absolutely on fire for him as he was for her. He took one pebbled nipple in his mouth, tempting her with his tongue and his teeth until her head fell back and her hips rolled against him. He held on to control by a thread, such a thin edge he knew he needed to bring her to completion now, because once he buried himself deeply inside her, restraint would be damn difficult to scavenge.

His hands glided down her spine, lowering her back as he kissed lower and lower still until she reclined along the piano. Her beautiful naked body sprawled on top of the sleek ebony grand took his breath away. Her hair trailed over the side of the piano in silken waves. He would never forget this picture of her as long as he lived. She was burned in his memory, on his soul.

He trekked along her body until he reached the core of her, damp and needy for him. He nudged her legs farther apart and nuzzled her essence, tasted her and teased her until her head thrashed back and forth. Her breathy moans of pleasure filled the air with a music that had seduced him then and now.

Her sighs grew to a crescendo that flowed through him, her back arching with the power of her release. He pressed a final kiss to her, then another against her stomach before he stood again.

And as the final ripples of aftershocks shivered through her, he scooped the condom from the corner of the piano and sheathed himself. Clasping her knees, he leaned over her and nudged inside, fully, deeply. He groaned at the total bliss of being exactly where he belonged. The warm clamp of her body gripping, pulsing around him nearly finished him before he could move, and oh, how much he wanted to move inside her. And move again, and again, filling her with each rocking thrust.

Her arms splayed, she gripped the sides of the piano to anchor herself to meet him, locking him more firmly with her legs around his waist. Guiding him. Holding him. With him every second of the way as she came undone with him all over again, their shouts of completion twining together.

Gasping with the power of what they'd shared, he leaned over her, blanketed her. He buried his face in her hair, their naked bodies slick and sealed with perspiration. With each steadying inhale of her sweet, floral scent, he knew.

Even if those threats against her evaporated in the morning, there wasn't a chance in hell he could let her go.

Celia sat naked on the silk sheets in Malcolm's bedroom, her body flushed and languid from making love on the piano. Against the wall. In the bed. In the shower.

Now they were in bed again. Or rather, she was. He'd stepped into the living area for the tray of cheese and fruit.

They'd stayed up most of the night, and not just making love. He'd brought his guitar into the room about halfway through the night and sang her the silliest made-up songs. She'd laughed until her sides ached, then taunted him by taking the guitar and composing her own ditties in return.

They would leave for London in the morning. She could sleep on the plane. For now, she intended to make the most of this night with Malcolm, because thinking about the future felt too uncertain, and she refused— absolutely refused—to do anything that would risk triggering a panic attack.

Angling to the side, she grasped the neck of his guitar and lifted it from the chair by the bed. She tucked it in place, scooped a pick from the bedside table and plucked through a riff of her own, not as intricate as his by any stretch, but she loved music. Loved that they shared this between them.

Their night together had been too perfect. Too special. She didn't want to think about threats at home or what the future held.

Malcolm strode through the door, gloriously naked and

all man. Muscles filled out his lean lines, sandy-brown hair dusting along his bronzed skin. He set a large silver tray in the middle of the bed, having added bottles of sparkling water to go with the food.

"What are you playing? An ode to my masterful… pick?"

"Ha, you're a comedian *and* a rock star. Imagine that." Laughing, she started to set aside the guitar.

He stopped her with a touch to the wrist. "Don't let me keep you from playing. I'm enjoying the music and the view."

"We can 'play' more later." She set aside the guitar and plucked free a handful of grapes. "Right now, I'm starving."

He settled beside her, careful not to tip the tray on the thick, downy comforter. "I'm sorry you didn't get to see more of Amsterdam. After we arrive in London tomorrow, we'll have an evening to ourselves, a day's break before two nights of concerts, then on to Madrid." He twisted open one of the chilled bottles and poured water into the two crystal glasses. "I feel bad that you haven't had much sightseeing or relaxation while we were in some of the most beautiful cities in the world. Choose whatever you want to do on the day off."

"More of what we're doing right now." She pressed a grape to his lips.

"No arguments from me." He bit free the fruit, nipping her fingers lightly.

Purring, she leaned forward to kiss him quickly, the sweet taste lingering on his mouth. "We'll lock ourselves in the hotel—"

"Actually, I have personal accommodations in London." He toyed with a lock of her hair, still damp from the shower they'd shared.

"Oh, that's right. Your mother has a flat there." She rocked back, taking her water glass, avoiding his eyes. Would Terri Ann be more open to her presence in Malcolm's life this go-round? If not, it could be quite awkward staying in an apartment together.

"I have a house in London, as well. I bought it to spend time with her when she's in town. We don't step on each other's toes." He grinned reassuringly. "Don't worry. I'm not taking you to my mother's place, where I would have to sneak into your room in the middle of the night."

Might as well meet this head-on. She didn't play games anymore. She wasn't an immature, spoiled teen. "Your mom has never been my biggest fan, and I get it. She was protective of you. And honestly, I admire how hard she worked to give you the best life possible." The town had never been short on gossip about the way Malcolm's father—a musician in a band—played a gig in Azalea, then cut out on his family. "The past and present can't help but be entwined."

"Remember how in fourth grade we had music class together? You were like magic at the piano, so happy when you played. You made the music come alive." He caressed down her arm to link fingers with her.

She laughed, squeezing his hand. "You played right alongside me, faster, trying to show me up. I recall that day well."

"No, I wanted you to notice me, so I figured I'd better step up my game. I'd mastered the technical side, but I missed the boat when it came to understanding music the way you did." He leaned back against the headboard, his glass resting on his bent knee.

"I never guessed." She blinked in surprise. "I thought you needed a duet partner for the talent show."

"You accomplished what all those music teachers had

been pounding their heads against the keyboard to make happen. I appreciate what my mother sacrificed for me, but all of this, the concerts, none of it would have happened without you."

A stint in reform school wouldn't have happened without her relentless pursuit of him, either, she thought wryly. She'd worked hard to change, but that didn't alter the past. He'd been so angry with her for insisting the baby be put up for adoption. Had he let that anger go? Or was it just set aside for now while the adrenaline and hormones worked to keep them both sated, relaxed?

She wondered if she could bring herself to ask him about it when their reunion was still so fresh, when only heaven knew how long it would last.

Instead, she drew circles on Malcolm's muscular chest. "You would have gotten there on your own. I was just in the right place when you were on the brink of understanding the music."

She remembered those days when Malcolm had catapulted from a skilled player to a talent to be reckoned with. She could almost see the music coming from his heart instead of his head when he'd been at the piano.

"Tell yourself whatever you want." He set aside his glass and hers, then gathered her against his chest.

In spite of all her good intentions five seconds ago, she couldn't stop herself from asking, "Why didn't you contact me after you got out? It's not like I was tough to find, hanging around our old hometown."

He rested his chin on top of her head. "I'd already wrecked your life once." His voice rumbled in his chest against her. "I was mature enough not to do an encore."

"But you're with me now because my life's in danger." Instead of shying away from the tough questions, she decided she deserved real answers. "Would you have stayed away forever?"

"Would *you?*" he countered.

Ouch. Good point. "You're a world-famous singer. I wouldn't have been able to get past your first line of body-guards. That security is why I'm here now, remember?"

"I wouldn't have turned you away." His arms wrapped tighter around her.

"It's not like we can even blame evil parents for keeping us apart. We did this to ourselves." She understood her reasons, if not his. "I've been punishing myself. Atoning for every mean-girl thing I ever did."

"Where the hell do you come up with this mean-girl notion?"

"I was a brat."

He tipped her chin up and stared at her with intensely blue eyes. "You were rebellious, funny, spoiled and absolutely magnificent. You still are."

"Spoiled?"

"Magnificent." He sealed the word with a kiss, nipping her bottom lip then nuzzling her ear. "I don't want this to end when the tour ends or even if all your father's enemies are locked up."

Stunned, she arched back, staring into his eyes. "You're serious."

She'd just managed to think about being with him tomorrow and now he was talking about longer.

"Absolutely serious," he answered. "Let's spend the summer together, explore what we're feeling and see where it takes us."

What about after the concert tour ended in four weeks? Where would they spend the rest of the summer? He'd avoided his hometown for nearly eighteen years. But the life she'd built there was a part of her, a part of who she was and the peace she'd found. She could enjoy this part of his life, but could he enjoy hers? Or did he only want the impulsive, bold girl she'd once been?

"What if I said I want to spend the rest of the summer in Azalea after your tour ends?" Why was she pushing when just that one question made her chest go tight? She didn't have to have the answers today.

"If that's where you want to be—" pausing, he cricked his neck from side to side "—I can stomach a few weeks there."

Stomach? Not a ringing endorsement for the safe life she embraced. "And in the fall?"

They were only delaying the inevitable crash, delaying the confrontation of the things that had made both of them choose to stay apart all these years. Her guilt over how she'd ruined their lives. His anger over her decisions. Her need for the stability of Azalea. His preference for luxury and travel.

Her feelings of betrayal because yes, damn it all, she'd expected him to come back for her a long time ago, but he'd chosen this life over her.

He moved the tray aside and took her hands. "This isn't going the way I intended. Do you need some kind of commitment from me? Some sign that you mean more to me than just a fling? I can do that."

That wasn't what she'd meant at all. Her heart fluttered in her chest, and it wasn't panic, but it was fear. What if he proposed and she said yes? Could she let go of the past and be with him? Could she live with the uncertainty and lavishness of his lifestyle after working so hard to create a stable existence? What if he was genuinely willing to live a regular, boring life with her when he wasn't on tour?

Was that even possible with his notoriety?

"Celia, I'm not just a musician."

"I know. You're also a gifted composer." She thought of the songs he'd written for her when they were younger, and even beyond that to the dozens of award-winning tunes he'd sent soaring up the charts over the years.

"That's not what I meant."

"Oh…" Disappointment and confusion swirled inside her. "What did you mean, then?"

He drew in a deep breath. "What I'm about to tell you can go no further, but I want you to know I trust you. That I'm committed."

There was that *commitment* word again.

"I work for Colonel Salvatore—" he paused "—and John Salvatore works for Interpol."

Eleven

Celia struggled to grasp what Malcolm had just told her, but what he'd shared seemed so unbelievable, so unexpected. He couldn't be serious. Except, as she looked at him, she saw he was completely sincere. He was some kind of secret agent.

"Interpol?" she asked, needing more details, needing some frame of reference for how this could be possible. "I'm really not tracking with what you're saying. You're going to need to help me understand."

"I'm trusting you with very sensitive information here. Salvatore manages a group of freelance operatives for Interpol. People he taps maybe once or twice a year for undercover help gathering evidence in an international criminal investigation. Because of my job, I move in some influential circles—some of them with shady ties. Having someone like me on the Interpol roll saves having to spend months building a cover."

As he explained, pieces shuffled in her mind. Other things began to make sense.

"That's how you knew about the threats against me. You have connections, intelligence connections." Her skin prickled with icy realization. "You've been watching me."

"Just keeping track of your life to make sure you're all right." He frowned. "That didn't sound right. Not in a stalking sort of way. More like a request to my boss that I be notified if you had a problem. The truth about my job isn't something I've told anyone other than you."

"Not even your manager? Or your friends?" All of his high-profile friends who had gone to Colonel Salvatore's school. Had they all gathered around to guard her? Or did they connect because they could discuss their common job? "Are they also freelance agents with high-profile lives—"

He kissed her silent. "Don't ask questions I'm not allowed to answer. I shared with you as much as I can to let you know I'm not taking what happened between us here lightly. This meant something to me. You mean something to me. I'm trusting you. Can you offer me some trust in exchange?"

His words so closely echoed ones they'd said to each other before, a replay of their past. He'd wanted her to trust that he could carve out a future for them. She'd needed him to trust her decision to give the baby up for adoption. In the end, they'd both gone their separate ways rather than risk being hurt.

They were older now, wiser. But they didn't seem to have a helluva lot more answers. As much as she wanted to lose herself in this time away from Azalea, it seemed her home and past just kept right on following her.

In fact, a huge part of that past waited for her in London when she saw his mother again.

* * *

After the flight to London, Malcolm drove his Aston Martin deeper in the rolling English countryside. He'd trusted Celia with a lot in Amsterdam, but that revelation hadn't gone as he'd expected. He'd hoped she would feel safer, that she would understand he was trying to welcome her into his world. Sharing the truth about his Interpol world had been a big step for him. Hell, admitting he still had feelings for her had been a giant leap.

And she'd reacted with silence and more silence. He could see the wheels turning but didn't have a clue what she was thinking. He could only hazard a guess. Was she upset over his hidden job? Worried? She didn't look as if she was having an anxiety attack.

He glanced at her sitting beside him in the silver sports car. "You've been quiet since we left Amsterdam."

She smiled over at him, her hair carrying on the breeze through the open window. "I thought men liked peace."

"Maybe I'm getting intuitive in my old age." He draped his wrist over the steering wheel, guiding the finely tuned machine along the curving two-lane road past an apple orchard.

"Or maybe you got those intuitive skills from your second job," she said as if joking, but not quite hitting the note.

"Freelancing for Interpol isn't nearly as intriguing as it sounds."

"Can you tell me anything about the cases?"

He weighed his words, wanting to give her what he could to bring her peace so they could move forward. He'd told her to make things easier between them, not more complicated. "Think of the corruption that goes on in the entertainment industry."

"Drugs?"

"I already have a built-in backstory on that one," he said darkly, thinking of his brush with the law as a teenager.

"Your partying lifestyle is a cover?"

"That's not what I meant." He took her palm in his, her dress silky against the back of his hand. "I haven't been a saint since I left home, but I do *not* touch drugs. I never would, especially not after what my father put my mother through."

"Your father was into drugs?" she asked, surprise lacing her voice.

"He was a meth addict." The admission burned, along with anger and betrayal. "He was the stereotypical stoned musician in a going-nowhere band. He blew through everything he and my mother had worked for. He would have sold his soul—or his family—for his next fix."

"Your mother's been through a lot." Celia's fingers gripped his tighter. "I'm sorry I put you in a position where you were forced to hurt her."

"Stop blaming yourself for everything that happened. I take responsibility for my own actions." He lifted her hand, kissing her knuckles. "You make me sound like I had no say in things. I wanted you. I would have done anything to have you in my life."

"Not anything..." she said softly, turning her head toward the open window as if the cottages and sheep were infinitely interesting.

"Hey." He tugged her hand until she turned back to him again. "What do you mean?"

"Nothing. Forget I said anything. So how much farther to this home of yours?"

He started to press her on the point, but then he noticed the nervous way she chewed at her thumbnail. She wasn't as calm as she pretended. He thought of her issues with anxiety and pulled back, saving the question for a better time.

"Not much farther. The gate's just beyond those trees." He crested the hill, revealing his home away from home for the past two years.

Celia gasped. "You leased a castle?"

He laughed. "Not a castle, actually—a manor house." A very large, brick manor house, restored but dating back to the seventeenth century. He wanted somewhere to escape the chaos around his L.A. home, and this small village called to him. "And, uh, it's not leased. I own it."

"And your mother has a flat in London. What would that be? Quarters in Buckingham Palace?"

"Not *in* the royal palace, but with a nice view of it." His mother had followed his father around for ten years while his dad played in bars and honky-tonks, dragging her son along, as well. When they reached Azalea, Mississippi, his mother had woken up the next morning to a note on the pillow. Apparently dragging a woman and kid around was killing the band. For a long time, Malcolm wondered if his mother would have left him behind if she'd been given the choice.

But she hadn't. And there was no denying she'd sacrificed everything for him and for his talent, even though his love of music had to be a hard pill for her to swallow given his father's proclivities. She'd made peace with it when she'd decided he would achieve the star power his father never had reached. He'd practiced to make her happy, to pay her back for costing her security.

He took his foot off the accelerator, coasting down the hill toward the gates covered with ivy. "My mother and I need our space after living in that crappy two-bedroom apartment for so many years."

"This is definitely…spacious."

"You disapprove?" He stopped outside the heavy iron gates, letting the security scan his irises.

She shook her head. "Your money is yours to spend. I'm just a bit overwhelmed by the scope of what you have."

He drove through, her reaction to the house he'd chosen far too important to him. "This is what I wanted to give you, a fairy-tale home."

"The sort of happily ever after you sing about." She grinned at him impishly.

He winced, downshifting around a curve on the winding driveway. "Not fair, turning my cynicism back on me, you know."

"Actually, I was being honest." She leaned out of the window, inhaling. "And oh, my goodness, there are flowers everywhere. It's truly a beautiful home."

Apparently she approved of the sculpted gardens he'd ordered with her in mind. He didn't know the names of most of the flowers. When he'd overseen the renovations, he'd just pointed to pictures in the landscaper's book, but he'd specifically requested climbing roses and lavender.

"I'm glad you like it." Pride kicked through him over pleasing her, having finally found the right way to romance this complex woman.

"Who wouldn't? The place is magnificent."

He wanted to press for more. Hell, when hadn't he wanted to push for more from Celia? He wasn't the most perceptive man on the planet, but something in her tone was still…off.

And opening some deep discussion right now didn't seem wise since his mother had just stepped out onto the lanai to greet them.

* * *

Celia dried her palms along her whispery red dress, sitting on the lanai beside Terri Ann Douglas and feeling the woman's eyes boring into her. Malcolm was parking the car and putting away their minimal luggage. Apparently, he'd had his mother arrange for everything else they would need here. Terri Ann had ordered the kitchen stocked, the beds fluffed. She'd given the main staff the weekend off, with only a catering service making very brief—discreet—stops by for meals.

"Um, Mrs. Douglas—"

"Terri Ann, please," his mother said nicely enough.

"Okay, Terri Ann, um…" She forgot what she was going to say.

God, this was awkward. She'd been semi-prepared to talk to the woman when she'd thought Malcolm was going to try to dump her on his mother back in the States. But she was totally unprepared for this visit now.

Perhaps because the memory of their night together was still so fresh in her mind and she was wondering how soon they could distract themselves with sex again. She trailed her fingers along the waist-high wall between her and those magnificent gardens with an angel fountain glistening in the late-afternoon sun. The scent carried on the air, and she couldn't even enjoy it because her stomach was in knots over this confrontation she should have seen coming. Malcolm's mother was here, serving up tea and sandwiches, for heaven's sake, as if the past didn't exist. As if they could erase the last time this woman had spoken to her.

Screamed, actually.

Crying and accusing her of wrecking Malcolm's life. So long ago.

Time had been kind to Terri Ann, smoothing the

edges. Her dark blond hair may have grayed somewhat, but her blue eyes were no longer tired with dark circles. She still favored cowboy boots and jean skirts. Did she also hold on to grudges?

Celia tried to smile, waving to the table of pretty little sandwiches, cakes and tea. "Thank you for going to so much trouble for me."

"No trouble at all. After all Malcolm does for me, the least I can do is help him out whenever he asks." She sat on one side of the stone table and served up a plate. "And he doesn't ask often."

Celia nibbled the edge of a cucumber sandwich. "Uh, thank you."

Damn, she sounded like a broken record.

"Malcolm will want something heartier from the pantry, but these seemed more ladylike for you."

Terri Ann thought she needed some kind of special airs put on? She just wanted to have an adult, comfortable conversation with the woman.

"I'm sorry." Celia set aside the delicate china plate carefully. "Would you mind if we use this time to clear the air before Malcolm arrives?

"I don't know what you mean." Terri Ann folded the napkin on her lap once and over again.

"You made it very clear eighteen years ago that you didn't approve of me." Celia pleated the hem of her dress between her fingers and hated that she betrayed her nerves this way. Hated even more how this woman made her feel sixteen and awful again. "I don't expect us to be best friends now just because Malcolm brought me here."

"That's good to know," Terri Ann said, giving little away. "I don't want to upset my son."

"And I don't intend to run telling tales to stir trouble. I

know you don't have any reason to trust me, but I'm not the same self-centered girl I was in those days."

"If we're being honest, then yes, you were spoiled, but my son made his own choices," Terri Ann conceded—surprisingly generous. "In the long run, you didn't ruin his life. Getting sent to that military boarding school was the best thing that ever happened to him. He got opportunities there I could never give him, no matter how many second jobs I took cleaning a salon or waiting tables."

Celia had certainly never thought of it that way. His sentence had seemed like just that…a sentence for a crime he didn't commit. She kept her silence as Terri Ann continued.

"Your father made that chance happen. He pulled strings with one of his judge cronies for Malcolm to go to that school rather than to jail or some crime-riddled reform school."

Celia wrestled with the shifting image of her past and the secrets her father had kept from her. Why hadn't he told her what he'd done for Malcolm? "My dad never told me. But then I was dealing with some pretty serious issues in those days."

She'd sunk into a depression during her pregnancy that had only deepened after the baby was born. The postpartum blues had spun out of control into a full-out breakdown. Putting the pieces of her life—of her sanity—together again had been a long, painful process.

Had her father just not wanted to risk her revisiting that time, even in memories? She might not have been strong enough to discuss the subject in the beginning, but she was now. And wow, how strange if felt to realize that about herself. To accept it. To let that confidence settle deep inside her.

Terri Ann smiled, thumbing a smudge of bright pink

lipstick from the corner of her mouth. "I won't deny I was glad you were no longer in my son's life. I know what it's like to be a parent too young, and I wanted him to have better than I was able to give him."

"But Malcolm turned out amazing. He's built an incredible life for himself." Did his mother know about the Interpol angle and just how far her son took being a good guy? "You did a good job bringing him up on your own."

"It was tough as hell, but I owed him for bringing him into this world. Do you think I wanted him to go through those same struggles, even younger than I was when I had him? At least I was nineteen when I had him." Terri Ann stared at her pointedly. "But then you certainly understand what I mean about making the best choice you can for your child. We can only do what we can with the resources we are given."

And here Malcolm's mother had shocked her all over again with support from an unexpected corner.

Terri Ann's smile faded. "Now, that doesn't mean we have to be best friends, like you said. I don't know you, the adult you. So as far as I'm concerned, let's both just start with a clean slate." Standing, she smoothed her denim skirt, picked up two sandwiches, carefully wrapping them in her napkin. "I'm going to leave you and Malcolm alone. Please tell my son I put some of his favorite barbecue in the fridge and a pecan pie on the counter."

Giving Celia the tour of his home had been satisfying and nerve-racking as hell. But so far, she liked the place. She'd sighed in appreciation over the antiques in the dining room. Spun a circle in the sunlight streaming through the domed conservatory. Sighed in bliss over the music room.

And he still wasn't any closer to finding out what had set her on edge after talking to his mother.

Perhaps it was time for a more direct approach. "What did you and my mom talk about?" he asked, leading her through the kitchen toward the steps to the cellar, where his favorite feature of the house waited.

"We talked about you, of course. She left you some of your favorite foods in the kitchen," she said, skimming her fingers along the cool stone walls of the narrowing corridor. Sconces lit the way with bulbs that resembled flickering flames. "And we discussed how you ended up at the military boarding school. How she felt like my dad did you a favor sending you there."

"Ohh-kay." That stunned him for at least two quick heartbeats before he said, "Not your average light chit-chat."

"Does she know about your Interpol work?" Her footsteps echoed behind him.

"No, I don't want to worry her." He glanced over his shoulder. "I meant it when I said telling you was a big commitment."

Her deep brown eyes stared back, still a little wary, confused even. Maybe he was moving too fast and should focus on how they communicated best. With sex. Really, really spectacular sex. Later, when she was ready, he could tell Celia that his feelings for her were about more than just the physical.

He stepped aside to reveal his latest treat for a woman he wanted to pamper with everything he'd earned over the years.

The old cellar enclosed a bubbling hot spring in the far corner. Except, it was more than a cellar. He'd reno-vated the space into a luxurious spa with modern conve-niences while preserving the historical feel. Weathered bricks, tan and ancient, lined the walls of the sprawling space. The natural spring had a deck of slick stones with steps leading down into the inviting waters. Steam rose toward fans hidden in the ceiling, the wafting heat attesting to the muscle-soothing promise those springs held.

Lounge chairs filled a corner by a wooden bar refurbished from an old pub. The bar had been outfitted with a refrigerator. On top, candles glowed alongside vases of flowers and a silver wine bucket holding a bottle of champagne—he'd placed that there himself. Some things, a man simply could not ask his mother to do.

The space provided the ultimate escape from the world for a man who had one helluva time finding peace and solitude. Intricately carved screens shielded a corner for changing, with fluffy robes and towels hanging on hooks buried into the walls.

Celia's gasp of pleasure mingled with the sound of trickling water. "This place is incredible."

"I looked at quite a few manor houses, even a couple of castles. But the minute I walked down here and saw the hot springs, I knew. This place would be mine." He knew this was the home he'd once dreamed of buying for Celia. And even thinking he would never be with her again, he'd still bought the place to remind himself of what they'd had. To remind him of the mission he had to make up for past mistakes.

"You renovated it, though, didn't you?" She eyed the sconces flickering on the wall and casting shadowy illumination.

"I had some help from a professional, but yes, I gave substantive input on what I wanted the place to look like. How did you know?" He pulled out the magnum of champagne and uncorked the bottle.

"I didn't know for sure until you just confirmed it. You have a great eye."

He filled a crystal champagne flute, then a second. "One of my friends recommended this guy who does great work renovating historic homes, blending the old with the new while still listening to the owner. I didn't want this to be some showplace for magazines that no real person would ever enjoy. I wanted this for me...for you."

"But you didn't know we would see each other again when you bought this home."

"And still, every decision I've ever made has been somehow tied to you." He passed the crystal flute to her, tiny bubbles fizzing to the top. "While we were dating, I used to make lists of all the things I would give you someday."

"I'm sorry I made you feel like I needed more." She sipped the champagne. "That wasn't fair to you."

"You were a teenager with parents—very wealthy parents—who loved you."

"Parents who spoiled me, you mean."

"I was a defensive teenager, full of pride and resenting like hell that I couldn't even drive you to the movies in my mom's old rust bucket of a car because she worked nights and needed it."

She tapped the edge of her glass to his. "What else was on that list?"

"Jewels. Houses. A car to make out in, a car that wasn't bought by your dad. And flowers." His slid his hand around a vase of fresh-cut roses on the bar. "An endless supply of fresh flowers."

"I love the flowers, outdoors and here."

"I had plans for those flowers over there." He pulled a creamy-white rose free from the vase.

"Like what?"

"Bed of petals upstairs. Bath with petals down here."
He plucked a handful of petals from the heavy bloom,
sprinkling them into the bubbling springs. "And always
with you naked."

"You, too, of course." She set her glass down along
the edge of the pool.

"That can be arranged."

Celia couldn't remember a time she'd peeled off her
clothes so quickly. Not since she and Malcolm had gone
skinny-dipping in the river near where they liked to park
and make out. Luckily, he was pitching aside his clothing
just as speedily before refilling their champagne glasses.

And placing a row of condoms along the ledge.

Smiling over her shoulder seductively, she walked
down the steps. The water was a hint too hot, then completely perfect for melting tensed muscles. Her quick
acclimation made her wonder if perhaps she'd been over-
thinking things. Maybe they could take this romance one
day at a time. Simply enjoy each other and unlimited sex,
making up for all the lost years when no one else came
close to touching her in that very special way.

The steaming water wrapped around her waist, lapping
higher and then teasing along her breasts until her nipples
beaded. The slick stone floor under her feet was warm
and therapeutic, as well. She hadn't expected even her
toes to feel pampered by the experience. Bubbles flowed
around her and under her, caressing her between her legs
and along her breasts erotically. Deliciously.

"Oh, my God, this is…just beyond what I could have
needed. Did you dump Xanax into the water?" She
winced at her own word choice, glancing at him sharply.
"Okay, that was a weak attempt at a joke."

"Was it some kind of Freudian slip?" His handsome face creased with concern.

She waded through the steam and over to him, standing toe to toe, needing to read his eyes as she spoke. "I have to know that you're not freaked out by the fact that I've had a breakdown. I have to know you're not going to handle me with kid gloves for fear I'll have a panic attack."

His hands fell on her shoulders, curving around to her back. "The urge to protect you is strong, and it was there long before you told me anything about medications or the stress after...the baby was born. I can't promise I won't go Cro-Magnon if someone threatens you. But I can promise I would have reacted the same way regardless."

With those few words, he wiped away her concern. "Good enough for me."

He walked backward, guiding her with him until he sat on a stone seat cut into the pool and pulled her into his lap. "When we were together before, I hated that I didn't have the cash to take you on real dates. I planned all the ways I would romance you when I had money."

"I treasured our time together. You put so much thought into what we did, just like you have here." She sipped her champagne, enjoying the tickle to her nose almost as much as she enjoyed the feel of Malcolm's muscular legs under her. "Even back then I knew what you did was tougher than tossing money around. Like the way you planted a sunflower at the spot where we first kissed."

"I stole a sunflower from the side of the road."

"It was sweet." She stroked back his stubborn lock of hair, teasing the familiar texture between her fingers. "Don't wreck the memory."

His hands slid up to cup her breasts, his thumbs teasing lazy circles until she beaded even harder against his touch. "I wanted to buy you flowers and take you to the homecoming."

"I don't care for football anyway. I just wanted to be with you." Sparks of pleasure shimmered from her breasts, gathering between her thighs. Wriggling to face him, she straddled Malcolm's lap, his hot, thick erection pressed between them. "Amazing, but I want that exact same thing from you now. More specifically, I want you to be inside me."

"You won't get an argument from me."

She reached past him for a condom, then slid her breasts along him, the bristle of his chest hair a tantalizing abrasion against her nipples. She sighed her pleasure, the head of his erection nudging against her, rubbing against the tight bundle of nerves aching for release.

With deliberate attention to detail, she sheathed him underwater, stroking the length of him and cradling his weight in her hands until his head fell back with a groan. She knew his body well again after their time in Amsterdam, but he'd been the one orchestrating their experience there. She savored being in control now.

"Celia, darlin', you're killing me..." His jaw flexed with restraint, muscles bunching and twitching. "Celia..."

"How much do you want me?" She angled closer, digging her fingers into the corded biceps bulging under her touch and rubbing their bodies against each other. Rubbing his erection between her cleft and against her stomach. But still she held herself back from giving them both what they wanted.

He growled, nipping her shoulder. "You know I want you more than I've ever wanted anyone."

"Do you know how many nights I laid awake thinking of you, your memory making me ache from wanting you? The sound of your voice over the radio in the morning would catch me unawares, leaving me needing you. Needing this."

She sank down, taking him deep inside her, fully and quickly. A raw groan of pleasure burst from his mouth, and she reveled in knowing he was every bit as helpless when it came to this attraction. She rolled her hips against his, arched her back for his attentive mouth on her breasts. Each flick of his tongue, every suckle followed by a puff of air drew the tension tighter inside her. He knew just how to play her body, strum her most sensitive spots, stroke and pluck just so until the need to come apart in his arms was almost painfully intense.

Water sluiced around them as they moved together, her arms locked tightly around him. The wall sconces flickered shadows over the hard planes of his face, teasing her with glimpses of his pleasure. His hands cupped her bottom, lifting and guiding her as he thrust upward. And her body answered, gripping him, holding him as pleasure built, higher until...

Fulfillment showered through her, sparkling through every fiber of her being. Gasping again and again with aftershocks rocking her, she scored Malcolm's shoulders, sinking in her nails as she held on. Her arms trembled. His grip tightened as he thrust faster and faster until, yes, he joined her.

And she held him close as his pleasure rocked through him, his breath hot on her neck, his beard a delicious abrasion against her temple as they clung to each other.

Even afterward, she stayed tangled with him, her legs wrapped around his waist now as she sat with him still inside her. Her skin cooled, even with the water steaming all around them. The lap of the bubbling tide stroking over her.

She gasped against the damp skin of his neck. She

wanted him, and God help her, she loved him, too. She always had.

But could she see this through with Malcolm, sign on for more? Could she live this out-of-control life with a man who played to sold-out arenas and royalty? Even if she could find her way around the anxiety of that lifestyle, there was the whole Interpol bombshell and his disdain for spending time in Azalea.

Desperately, she wanted to find a way through this crazy maze of a life he'd built for himself. An amazing life, without question, but it wasn't hers. It wasn't even close to what she wanted for herself... Well, maybe the spa part could stay....

God, she was a mess. She needed to find a path they could walk together.

Because if she didn't, staying with him only prolonged the inevitable, increasing the pain of losing Malcolm all over again.

Twelve

Malcolm sprawled in a chair on the lanai, brunch having been set up by a service his mother had arranged to make discreet appearances and speedy exits throughout their brief stay. He scrolled through his email while waiting for Celia to finish her shower.

Celia.

His hand slowed on the tablet, his eyes scanning the elaborate garden he'd had planted for her, not even knowing if she would ever see it. His gaze settled on a rose bush climbing along an archway over a bench. How many times over the past couple of years had he envisioned her there reading or singing? She'd been with him in his every thought over the years, every decision he made guided by what he'd wanted to give her.

Whatever it took, wherever his manager told him he needed to be to advance his career, he'd done it. He realized now that he'd done all this for her. He'd been keeping track of her because he wanted her back in his life. Protecting her had just been an excuse. He was so close to having what he'd dreamed of as a heartbroken kid. But he refused to let the surge of victory distract him from remembering his duty—making sure she stayed out of harm's way until Salvatore could get a lock on who'd left those threatening notes.

"Good morning." Celia smiled in the open French doors, the sun shining on her dusky beauty. Her hair glided over her shoulder in a side ponytail.

She strolled through the door. Her simple sundress, long and vibrantly blue, caressed her legs as she walked closer. Her hand glided over his chest as she dipped to kiss him, a hint of rose-petal perfume still clinging to her skin with reminders of how they'd made love in the spa for hours. If only they could block out the world awhile longer.

Protective urges surged through him, and he wondered why the hell it was proving so difficult to track down the person responsible for threatening Celia. He forced his fists to unclench and then stroked her ponytail. "Good morning to you, too, beautiful. Brunch? There's plenty."

He pulled out a chair for her at the table set with a full English fry-up of eggs, bacon, sausages, fried bread and mushrooms.

Celia bypassed it all, picking up a scone and a small pot of lemon curd as she took her seat. She swept the hem of her dress to the side as she settled in a move so utterly feminine it had him wanting to carry her out into the garden and make love to her all over again.

Except, then he noticed her brow was furrowed.

"What's wrong?" he asked, returning to his side of the table.

She slathered lemon curd on a corner of her scone.

"I'm still trying to piece together all the new things I'm learning about you, fill in the gaps of those years we missed."

"Such as?" he asked warily. He wanted to let her into his world, yet he wasn't a man used to talking about himself. He'd grown accustomed to keeping people at arm's length.

"I know you can't tell me about your friends and details about Interpol, but what about your time at school? Those early days when we were apart?"

He wasn't sure why she wanted to know, but he couldn't see the harm in sharing. "We weren't the typical button-up types who planned to go into the military. We banded together to get through, formed a new family since ours had been taken away. We broke rules, pushed boundaries. We called ourselves The Alpha Brotherhood, and in the confines of those prisonlike walls, we kept each other from losing our minds."

"You said you broke the rules—like when Elliot Starc hot-wired the truck?"

"Exactly." He speared food onto his plate. "One night, Troy broke into the security system, rewired the whole thing so Conrad's ankle monitor wouldn't register. We left school grounds, bought pizza and came back."

Laughing, she thumbed a crumb from the corner of her mouth, reminding him of all the ways she'd driven him crazy with those lips the night before. "Real rebels."

He cleared his throat. "It's like counting coup."

"Counting coup?" She broke off another bite of the scone, her attention to his words so intent it was as if the world hinged on what he would share.

"Mental games, war games—sneak into the enemy camp and leave a sign that you were there. Show your enemy their security is worthless." His mind filled with memories of how sweet those victories had tasted then as he'd lashed out at the world. "No need to destroy anything. Just let them know you're able to come and go as you please, that you can dismantle the whole system if you choose. Makes sticking around a lot easier."

"And your headmaster, this man who now works for Interpol, Colonel Salvatore. He was the enemy?"

"Back then he was, yes. And sneaking one past him was the ultimate victory for a group of teens who were feeling they'd been kicked in the teeth by the world." Little had they known then it was all a part of Salvatore's strategy to get them to work together as a unified team.

"What made you change your mind and join him?" Cradling a china teacup in her hands, she eyed him over the rim.

Malcolm set aside his silver fork with a clatter. "Turns out he was better at war games than we were. He found my weakness and he used it."

"I'm not sure I understand." She set her cup back on the saucer carefully and reached for her scone. "What did he do?"

His mind filled with memories of that fateful meeting when John Salvatore had approached him with the Interpol offer, when he'd revealed all the power that could be his if he just said yes, the power to keep track of Celia. The power to know…everything. A mixed blessing.

"He showed me pictures of our daughter."

Celia's scone crumbled in her hands, her fingers clenching too hard as shock sliced clean through her at Malcolm's words. At what he'd known all this time and never said a word about. He'd never offered her the consolation such information could have given her.

Her hands shaking, she dusted the crumbs from her

fingers and willed herself not to jump to conclusions, to be logical and hear him out.

"You had access to…things like that?"

He looked down at his uneaten food. "I haven't seen her in person or made contact. I honored the decision we made to leave that up to her."

The old ache inside her swelled. So painful. So empty.

She squeezed her eyes closed and blurted out, "I know you blame me for giving her up for adoption."

So much for the calm, logical approach.

"Celia? Celia," he insisted, taking her hand until she opened her eyes. "I signed the paperwork. I accept responsibility for my own decisions. I was in no position to be a parent stuck states away in a boarding school for misfits. It would have been selfish of me to put her life on hold waiting for me to get out."

"Then why haven't you forgiven me? Why can't we just be happy?"

"I have regrets. That's not the same as holding a grudge." He squeezed her hand in a reassurance that didn't quite warm the chill spreading inside her. "Do I wish things had turned out differently? Of course. I wanted to be the man who could take care of you both."

A whisper of suspicion curled through her like steam from the teapot. "Is that what all of this has been about? Coming to my rescue now to make up for what you think you should have done eighteen years ago?"

"In part, yes," he said, confirming her fear that things could never be simple for them, not after everything that came before. A fresh start for them wasn't an option. Malcolm leaned forward on his elbows. "What did she look like when she was born?"

"Didn't your Interpol connection give you photos from the nursery?" she snapped, then paused, holding

up a hand. "Sorry for being defensive. She looked...
wrinkled with her face scrunched up. She had dark hair
and the softest skin. I wanted her." Her breath caught in
her throat, every word slicing her like razor cuts on an
ache that had never fully healed.

She shoved back from the table, needing air, space. "I
really wanted her, and all my life I'd gotten everything I
wanted. But something changed inside me when I looked
in her eyes. I knew that as much as I wanted to keep her,
I couldn't give her what she needed on any level."

She shot to her feet, desperate to escape the painful
memories and the accusation she knew she would find
in Malcolm's eyes. "I can't do this. Not now."

Tears blurring her view of the two roses on the table,
she started toward the French doors.

"Her name is Melody," he said, his voice raw.

She stopped in her tracks, hardly daring to believe
what she'd heard. Bracing her hand on the open door,
her back to him, she said, "Her adoptive parents asked
me what I'd been calling her. I didn't expect they would
keep the name."

"They did. The photo I saw of her was taken when she
was seven years old—the only photo I saw—but even
then, she looked like you."

She clapped her hands over her ears. "Stop. If she
wants to find us, she will. That's her choice. We agreed."

"I can make this happen, though." He shoved to his
feet, closed the space between them in two strides and
clasped her shoulders. "We're a couple now. We can get
married and reach out to her."

"I meant it when I said that has to be her decision. I
owe her that choice." She blinked fast, her head whirling as her heart squeezed tight. She didn't want him to
ask for old times' sake or some need to make up for the

past. "And that proposal of yours was every bit as abrupt as when you asked me before when we were teenagers."

His eyes snapped with frustration. "And you're shutting me down just as fast."

"You're changing my life." She eased his hands from her shoulders. "You have to accept I'm not a reckless, impulsive teenager anymore. I have a life I'm proud of and have no interest in abandoning. I'm not cut out for this high-octane lifestyle of yours—the concert tour or the Interpol implications. God, Malcolm, think. We can't jump into this."

"Admit it. This isn't about where we live or what we do. It's about making a commitment to me." He took a step back, face stony with disillusionment, a replay of the way he'd looked at her so long ago. "You don't want to try now any more than you did then."

Why couldn't he understand she wasn't pushing him away, just looking for a compromise? "That's not true. You aren't even trying to see my side of this. And damn it, Malcolm, I am different now. I refuse to let you tear my heart out again."

Her chin high, her pride all she had left, she spun away and almost slammed into his mother in the doorway. Could this humiliating, heartrending moment get any worse? To hell with pride. She needed to get out of here.

Celia angled past with a mumbled "Excuse me," then ran. Her sandals slapped against the sleek wooden floors as she raced into the restored manor house. She ran up the curved staircase and into the bedroom full of antiques, florals and stripes. She slammed the door closed and sagged back against the panel only to realize...

She wasn't alone in the room.

A broad-backed male spun away from her suitcase, her tote bag in one hand, a piece of paper in the other.

"Adam Logan?" She walked toward Malcolm's manager. "What are you doing in my room?"

Her eyes went to the paper in his hand, a typed note with big block letters she'd seen on threatening notes over the past couple of weeks. Block letters that even from here she could read.

WATCH YOUR BACK, BITCH.

Malcolm scrubbed a hand over his face, trying to pull himself together before he spoke to his mother. God only knew how much of that train wreck of an argument she'd overheard. "Mom? What are you doing back here? Did you need something?"

"Actually, I was hoping to talk to you and Celia, but maybe this isn't the best time." His mother hovered uncertainly in the doorway.

"No, Mom, it's fine. Celia and I both could use some time to cool off." Although eighteen years of cooling off hadn't helped them. "Come sit down. Have a scone."

"If you're sure." She cleared the door, her yellow leather boots clicking across the tile lanai.

He moved Celia's plate aside as his mother sat. "What's on your mind?"

"I've been letting you support me for long enough," she said in a rush, as if she'd been holding the words inside.

What the hell? Who tipped the world upside down while he wasn't looking? "Mom, that's ridiculous. I owe you. I *want* to give you these things—anything you need."

"You're my son." She patted his arm. "It was my job to take care of you. You don't owe me anything."

"Damn it, Mother, the money doesn't even make a

dent in my portfolio. I don't miss it." He could have retired from the concert scene years ago.

"That's beside the point," she said primly, folding her hands in her lap.

"To you maybe. But not to me. I can't watch you work that hard ever again." Years of guilt piled on top of him, so much he didn't know how he would ever dig out. "I just can't."

"Well, I'm not looking to embrace abject poverty." She laughed lightly. "I've gotten used to the softer side of life. But maybe a little too used to it."

"What do you mean?" He tried to sort through her words, really tried, because apparently he'd been missing the mark with both of the women in his life.

She took a deep breath, as if bracing herself, then said, "Do you think that monstrously large bank account of yours could handle sending your old mother to school? I'd like to become a professional caterer, one who specializes in entertaining on a budget. When I said I've become accustomed to the softer side of life, I meant it. I'd like to bring those treats and delicacies to others who never thought they could afford them."

He was stunned, to say the least. But the plan she'd spelled out made perfect sense. The pieces fit, and he was happy for her. "Mom, I think that's a great idea. But I'm still curious. What brought this big turnaround?"

"Seeing you with Celia in the news, hearing all the reports about what she's been doing with her life. She could have relied on her father's money, but she carved out a place for herself in the world. That's admirable, son."

His mother was right. Celia had. And she was clearly stronger for that, more confident. She'd been telling him she wasn't the selfish, spoiled girl he'd once known, but had he actually understood? Accepted? He forced himself to focus on his mother's words. Apparently a man never got too old to learn something from his mom.

"Malcolm, those pictures the press has been running of her with students showed how much she loves her profession. This may sound strange, but I never considered that work could be fulfilling. The jobs I did before, I took pride in them, sure, but they were just a means to put food in your mouth. And there weren't a lot of choices. I have a choice now, thanks to you—"

A scream split the air.

Celia's voice.

What the hell?

Malcolm shot from his chair, toppling it as he sprinted for the stairs. Celia's screams continued, mixed with masculine shouts. His gut clenched with fear. Where were the guards? Why hadn't security been triggered? What the hell had he been thinking lowering his own guard with her just because he had her an ocean away from the threat?

He raced through the door and barely had time to register what he was seeing. Celia held a huge vase of flowers high and crashed it down on the head of…

Adam Logan?

His manager?

Logan's knees buckled, and he fell to the ground.

Malcolm barked, "What the hell's going on here? Celia, are you okay?"

She backed away, pointing at his manager, now kneeling in a puddle of water, shattered glass and roses on the thick Persian rug. "He was in my room, going through my things. He had a threatening note and a dead rose. He was putting it in my bag."

Malcolm turned to Logan, a man he'd called his friend,

his brother. "Adam? You were the one behind the threats on Celia? Why the hell would you do that?"

Logan sagged back on his heels, his shoulders slumping forward. "I just wanted to get the two of you together again."

It made no sense. Malcolm looked to Celia, who appeared just as confused. He wanted to drape an arm around her, tuck her close, but she stood quietly on the other side of the room.

"You'd better explain. And fast." His pulse pounded beneath his eye, anger roiling.

Logan leaned forward, his eyes gleaming with the cutthroat, ambitious light that had helped push Malcolm's career to the limit. "Your bad-boy image was starting to drag on your numbers. And you have to admit, we got a lot of good press out of the high-school-sweethearts-reunited angle. It was easy enough to pull off, then make sure Salvatore heard." He shrugged. "It's actually sort of funny when you think about it, pulling off a prank on the old colonel again."

Malcolm wasn't laughing. This bastard had terrified Celia for absolutely no good reason. Already brimming with frustration from his fight with Celia, Malcolm couldn't stem the anger for a second longer. He hauled back his fist and punched Logan square in the jaw.

His manager crumpled back onto the rug, out cold. A formality, actually, since Celia had clearly handled things on her own. She stood strong and magnificent, in control of the situation.

His thoughts synched up in that moment as the truth truly sank in. Celia could take care of herself. As his mother had said, Celia had built the life that she wanted. He was the one still chasing the past, trying to change the outcome or hide from the tougher parts. Like how he'd stayed away from Azalea and Celia rather than face up to his feelings. Rather than risk putting his heart on the line again.

She had every reason to be angry with him. He'd failed to acknowledge the strong and incredible woman she'd become, the completion of the dazzling young girl he first fell for. The woman he still loved.

If he didn't figure out how to get his priorities in order, he didn't stand a chance of winning her back. And losing wasn't an option. He loved this woman with every fiber of his being. Every note he played, every breath he took was for her. Always for Celia.

Whatever it took, he would be the man worthy of spending his life with her.

As Celia stood in the back of the concert hall that night, her mind was still reeling from the shock of finding Malcolm's manager in her room. Of learning he'd been behind those threats all along. Adam Logan had orchestrated everything as a way to get Malcolm some extra publicity. Her life had been horribly manipulated.

But the frustration and anger she experienced had to be nothing compared to the disillusionment Malcolm felt over his friend's betrayal. There hadn't been time to talk after the attack. Malcolm had been so focused on dealing with the crisis at hand that she'd been shut out as the mess in front of her was "handled." He'd made the decision to contact Salvatore and let him wade through the legal ramifications. The press from this, however, would be rough on Malcolm—betrayed by his own manager.

For that reason, she'd been unable to leave right away. In honor of all she and Malcolm had shared, in the past and in the present, she would stay for tonight's concert. If Adam Logan had been correct, that she'd been good press for Malcolm, she would at least give him this night to help smooth over the rough patch he was bound to face with the media. And after he sang that last encore?

She honestly didn't know. She just wished she had some kind of sign as to what she should do next. Marry Malcolm and change her life? Or return to what she'd had?

From the back of the auditorium, she watched him perform, her eyes riveted by his mesmerizing charisma. The audience hung on his every note, his every word. His performance was as smooth as ever, even though he couldn't play the piano or guitar tonight. He'd broken two fingers punching out his manager. Sometime during the chaotic day, a doctor had been called to splint Malcolm's fingers just before he left for the sound check.

In fact, his concert was beyond phenomenal tonight. She couldn't put her finger on the difference. Her eyes scanned the sold-out historic theater. The space resembled the Amsterdam venue. The acoustics of the old building were formidable, but not the best she'd heard. Nothing had changed with the lighting. Yet, still…tonight *was* different. Exponentially better in some undefinable way.

Perhaps the fact that this was a charity benefit added something to his performance? She smoothed her hands down her floor-length red satin gown, feeling a bit like Cinderella at the ball with midnight only seconds away. Certainly, Malcolm looked heart-stoppingly handsome in his tuxedo. As the concert rolled to a close, she realized he didn't intend to sing "Playing for Keeps." Although, how could she blame him after the grief she'd given him the last time he'd performed it? She'd chewed him out for selling fans a fake bill of goods, crooning to them with lyrics he didn't believe in.

And then, as he finished the final ballad of the night,

sitting on a bar stool and singing directly to the audience, she grasped the difference in tonight's show. The difference in Malcolm.

He *wasn't* performing.

Tonight when he sang about love won and lost, love's pain and joy, she would swear he really believed the words. That had to be it. He felt the emotion, believed in love and happily ever after. The feelings were so real they shone from his eyes. His proposal earlier hadn't sprung from some gut reaction or need to protect her. Somehow Malcolm's faith in happily ever after had been restored. He'd come to believe in it again. This was the sign she'd been waiting for. She'd thought his proposal was for old times' sake or to make up for the past.

And she'd thrown his proposal back in his face.

Her heart squeezed tight with emotion as she realized how very badly she'd messed up, and how every second that passed was filled with pain neither of them should have to endure. They'd both been through enough. They'd sacrificed and lost too much because of their mistakes. They'd made amends.

They deserved to be happy.

Hitching up the hem of her floor-length gown, she sprinted back out into the lobby, searching for the back-stage entrance and regretting like hell that she'd refused the backstage pass earlier out of fear. Out of some contrary need to put up walls between them.

She ran toward the guards at the doors, and thank God, one of them remembered her and waved her through with a wink and a smile. He even pointed the way. High heels clicking along the concrete floors, she dashed past crates and music stands, endless equipment crowding her path. Finally, she made it to the wings, stopping beside the stage manager, who held up a finger to his lips.

Although with the loud applause as Malcolm bowed, it wasn't as if anyone could hear her.

Celia nodded anyway, breathless from her mad dash. Her heart pounded in her ears with anticipation and hope. Malcolm had already started to exit the stage, walking toward her. Although he hadn't seen her yet since he still waved to the audience, already on their feet clapping.

Malcolm stepped out of the lights and into the darkened wings, his hand already out for the customary bottled water the backstage assistants would pass him before he returned for an encore.

Celia thrust out her hand with a water bottle, their fingers brushing.

Sparks flying as always.

Malcolm halted in his tracks. "You're here."

"Where else would I be?" she said simply. She didn't bother weighing her words to preserve her pride. What a silly emotion anyway. "I love you, so I'm here."

The stage manager covered his grin.

Malcolm clasped her arm and guided her away—the stage manager's smile quickly shifting to panic as Malcolm tucked her in a private corner of storage containers.

"Celia, did I hear you right?" He set the water aside, his focus solely on her.

"I meant every word, and I'm sorry I didn't say it earlier instead of running."

He hauled her close and held her tightly. "Oh, God, Celia, I love you, too," he whispered in her hair. "I always have."

Although she knew that already. She'd heard it in his voice with every word he sang. Still, it was so very good to hear him say it plainly.

He angled back, cupping her face. "I'm sorry I let so many years go by without reaching out to you. I let pride get in the way of us having a chance at fixing the past, of building a future. And most of all, I apologize for not trusting you now, for not listening to what you want for your life. For not believing what's right in front of me."

"What might that be?" She skimmed the overlong lock away from his forehead.

"You fascinated the hell out of me eighteen years ago. But you absolutely mesmerize me now. You are an incredible woman, stunning, independent. And so damn giving I can't figure out what I did to deserve this second chance with you."

The pounding of the audience stomping the floor for another song was nothing compared to her heartbeat in her ears. "It's time we both believe and trust that we deserve to be happy. We deserve a future together."

"Darlin', I do like the way you think." He sealed his mouth to hers, a sure and perfect fit. He finished with a kiss on her nose before he rested his forehead against hers. "What would you say to my retiring?"

The stage manager hovered, but Malcolm waved him off.

"From Interpol? I know what Adam Logan did hurt you—"

He shook his head. "That's not what I meant. What if, after this tour, I retired from the stage."

"I'm…stunned."

He searched her eyes. "Good stunned or bad stunned?"

"I'm just surprised. I thought you lived for your music." She pointed toward the stage, the audience still on their feet applauding for their encore. "They live for your music. And tonight, the heart you put into your songs propelled you to another level."

"Celia, it's about you. It's always been about you. I've been chasing success to prove something to your father, to you—to myself—that really doesn't matter. I've learned so much from you these past several days... I want to compose music, and I have the financial luxury of never working again if I choose."

Wow, he really meant it. This wasn't some half-baked idea. He'd found his direction. And the fact that he attributed that to her meant more than she could say.

"Malcolm, your fans are going to grieve."

"There are plenty of singers more than ready to step into any void I might leave on the charts."

"You're really serious."

"Absolutely. I was approached not too long ago about writing a score for a movie, a sprawling postapocalyptic saga with an edgy vibe of modern-day meets classical—Adam advised me not to..." He hung his head briefly, then drew in a deep breath, meeting her eyes again. "I can do that anywhere, even in Azalea."

"Or there and here," she offered in compromise. "We could live in Azalea and London. I could still teach privately, work on a series of music books for students."

"That sheet music I saw in your office the first day..."

"Sounds like we're building a plan, together. And we can fine-tune the details later, because right now, you have a concert to finish."

His eyes glinted with an idea. "What do you say we give them their encore?"

Laughing, she rolled her eyes. "They're calling for you."

"Crazy, I know, but I don't want to let you go." He reached for a guitar. "Maybe you could play since I can't. We could sing together, like we used to. We can be a team, you and I."

Without hesitation, she hooked her arm in his and let him escort her out onto the stage. The crowd went wild at the sight of her. And when Malcolm took her hand as she settled on the bar stool, the crowd held their breath in anticipation. Celia looked out at the audience and saw his mother beaming from the front row. Celia smiled back before settling the guitar in her lap and turning to Malcolm.

Sharing a microphone with him, her heart in her eyes, she strummed the opening chords to "Playing for Keeps," the notes committed to memory years before. The melody was already a part of her heart.

* * * * *

REQUEST YOUR FREE BOOKS!

2 FREE NOVELS PLUS 2 FREE GIFTS!

HARLEQUIN®

Desire

ALWAYS POWERFUL, PASSIONATE AND PROVOCATIVE

YES! Please send me 2 FREE Harlequin Desire® novels and my 2 FREE gifts (gifts are worth about $10). After receiving them, if I don't wish to receive any more books, I can return the shipping statement marked "cancel." If I don't cancel, I will receive 6 brand-new novels every month and be billed just $4.30 per book in the U.S. or $4.99 per book in Canada. That's a savings of at least 14% off the cover price! It's quite a bargain! Shipping and handling is just 50¢ per book in the U.S. and 75¢ per book in Canada.* I understand that accepting the 2 free books and gifts places me under no obligation to buy anything. I can always return a shipment and cancel at any time. Even if I never buy another book, the two free books and gifts are mine to keep forever.

225/326 HDN FVP7

Name	(PLEASE PRINT)

Address	Apt. #

City	State/Prov.	Zip/Postal Code

Signature (if under 18, a parent or guardian must sign)

Mail to the **Harlequin® Reader Service:**
IN U.S.A.: P.O. Box 1867, Buffalo, NY 14240-1867
IN CANADA: P.O. Box 609, Fort Erie, Ontario L2A 5X3

Want to try two free books from another line?
Call 1-800-873-8635 or visit www.ReaderService.com.

* Terms and prices subject to change without notice. Prices do not include applicable taxes. Sales tax applicable in N.Y. Canadian residents will be charged applicable taxes. Offer not valid in Quebec. This offer is limited to one order per household. Not valid for current subscribers to Harlequin Desire books. All orders subject to credit approval. Credit or debit balances in a customer's account(s) may be offset by any other outstanding balance owed by or to the customer. Please allow 4 to 6 weeks for delivery. Offer available while quantities last.

Your Privacy—The Harlequin® Reader Service is committed to protecting your privacy. Our Privacy Policy is available online at www.ReaderService.com or upon request from the Harlequin Reader Service.

We make a portion of our mailing list available to reputable third parties that offer products we believe may interest you. If you prefer that we not exchange your name with third parties, or if you wish to clarify or modify your communication preferences, please visit us at www.ReaderService.com/consumerchoice or write to us at Harlequin Reader Service Preference Service, P.O. Box 9062, Buffalo, NY 14269. Include your complete name and address.

HD13

Vincenzo Arsenio D'Agostino stared at his king and reached the only logical conclusion.

The man had lost his mind.

Ferruccio Selvaggio-D'Agostino—the bastard king, as his opponents called him—twisted his lips. "Do pick your jaw off the floor, Vincenzo. No, I'm *not* insane. Get. A. Wife. ASAP."

Dio. He'd said it again.

Mockery gleamed in Ferruccio's eyes. "I've needed you on this job for *years,* but that playboy image you've been cultivating is notorious. And that image won't cut it in the leagues I need you to play in now. When you're representing Castaldini, Vincenzo, I want the media to cover only your achievements on behalf of the kingdom."

Vincenzo shook his head in disbelief. "*Dio!* When did you become such a stick in the mud, Ferruccio?"

"If you mean when did I become an advocate for marriage and family life, where have you been the last four years? I'm the living, breathing ad for both. And it's time I did you the favor of shoving you onto that path."

"What path? The one to happily-ever-after? Don't you know that's a mirage most men pursue until they drop in defeat?"

Ferruccio went on, "You're pushing forty…"

"I'm thirty-eight!"

"…*and* you've been alone since your parents died two decades ago…"

"I have friends!"

"…*whom* you don't have time for and who don't have time for you." Ferruccio raised his hand, aborting his interjection. "Make a new family, Vincenzo. It's the best thing you can do for yourself, and incidentally, for the kingdom."

"Next you'll dictate the wife I should 'get.'"

"If you don't decide, I will." Ferruccio gave him his signature discussion-ending smile. "'Get a wife' wasn't a request. It's a royal decree."

But Vincenzo knew it wouldn't be that easy. Like his king, Vincenzo had been a one-woman man. Unlike his king, he'd blown his one-off shot on an illusion.

Even after six years, the memory of her sank its tentacles into his mind, making his muscles feel as if they'd snap….

A realization went off in his head like a solar flare.

A smile tugged at his lips, fueled by what he hadn't felt in six years. Excitement. Anticipation.

All he needed was enough leverage against Glory Monaghan to make his proposal an offer she couldn't refuse.

Will Glory say yes?

Find out in

TEMPORARILY HIS PRINCESS by Olivia Gates.

*Available May 2013 from Harlequin® Desire
wherever books are sold!*

HARLEQUIN®
Desire

ALWAYS POWERFUL, PASSIONATE AND PROVOCATIVE.

THE RETURN
OF THE SHEIKH

by Kristi Gold

Sheikh Zain Mehdi has returned to his country—
a stranger in a familiar land—and he needs to shed
his bad-boy reputation. Enter political consultant
Madison Foster. Zain finds he doesn't want her
advice on how to be a good king, but he does want
her…. Playing with fire never felt so good.

Look for

THE RETURN OF THE SHEIKH
next month from Harlequin Desire!

Available wherever books are sold.

Powerful heroes…scandalous secrets…burning desires.

HD73243